Won't You Stay, Radhika?

रुकोगी नहीं, राधिका

Usha Priyamvada

Translated by
Daisy Rockwell

SPEAKING TIGER

SPEAKING TIGER BOOKS LLP
125A, Ground Floor, Shahpur Jat, near Asiad Village,
New Delhi 110049

Published in English in paperback by Speaking Tiger Books 2023
Originally published in Hindi as *Rukogi Nahi Radhika* in 1967

ISBN: 978-93-5447-590-0
eISBN: 978-93-5447-581-8

10 9 8 7 6 5 4 3 2 1

Typeset in Garamond Premier Pro by SÜRYA, New Delhi
Printed at HT Media Ltd, Greater Noida

Usha Priyamvada was born in 1930 in Kanpur, and earned her MA and PhD in English literature from Allahabad University. After teaching at Lady Shri Ram College for Women for three years and Allahabad University for two, Usha won a Fulbright fellowship to study comparative literature at the University of Indiana. Following that, she was hired at the University of Wisconsin, Madison, where she went on to teach for decades, until her retirement in 2002. Her teaching areas included Hindi, Modern and ancient Indian literature, Indian Folklore and Modern Hindi cinema, with a focus on women's empowerment. She has published seven novels, a study of Surdas, and numerous short stories, as well as articles on Hindi literature in English and a translation of the poetry of Mira Bai in English.

Daisy Rockwell is a painter, writer and translator living in Vermont, USA. She holds a PhD in South Asian literature from the University of Chicago, and wrote her doctoral thesis on the Hindi author Upendranath Ashk. She has translated Krishna Sobti's novel, *A Gujarat Here, a Gujarat There* (2019), as well as a number of other works, including Bhisham Sahni's *Tamas* (2016), Ashk's *Falling Walls* (2015), Khadija Mastur's *The Women's Courtyard* (2018), and Usha Priyamvada's debut novel *Fifty-five Pillars, Red Walls* (2021). Her translation of Geetanjali Shree's *Tomb of Sand* (2018) became the first novel translated from an Indian language to win the International Booker Prize in 2022. Daisy has also translated numerous short stories and poems which have appeared in journals such as *Asymptote*, *The Brooklyn Rail*, *Out of Print*, and *The Indian Quarterly*.

Introduction

> *For her, life was as cold as an attic with a window looking to the north, and ennui, like a spider, was silently spinning its shadowy web in every cranny of her heart.*
>
> —Gustave Flaubert, *Madame Bovary* (1857)

When we think of ennui, we laugh. Trust the French, we think, to privilege boredom as an emotion. We think of old French movies with very little plot, of people in black turtlenecks chain smoking in cafes, and symbolist poets so wracked by boredom, it brings them close to death. When we say, in English, 'to die of boredom,' it's hyperbolic, even humorous, but in French 'c'est à mourir d'ennui,' the same phrase, really, it is a more serious statement. We know ennui to be something greater than boredom: one of those special words that must be imported wholesale into English, like schadenfreude or dharma or hara-kiri. Just look at Emma Bovary! Flaubert's famous heroine suffers an ennui so stifling, she tries to stamp it out first with romance novels, then getting married, and finally, a series of disastrous affairs.

Nothing fits the bill and eventually (spoiler!) she poisons herself, literally dying of boredom.

Part of the divergence between the English word, boredom, and the French word, ennui, is that ennui actually means more than just boredom. In the plural, for example, it means troubles: 'j'ai des ennuis' means 'I've got problems,' not 'I have more than one thing that's boring me.' Ennui carries with it the sense of something weightier than boredom. In fact, ennui can be a serious affliction. In another quintessentially ennui-drenched French novel, *Bonjour Tristesse* (1954) by Françoise Sagan, the narrator, Cécile, explains, 'A strange melancholy pervades me to which I hesitate to give the grave and beautiful name of sorrow.' Melancholy, a close kin to sorrow or depression, is another valence to the experience of ennui.

Why, you may be wondering, is this translator writing about a French concept to introduce her translation of a Hindi novel? A good question! This is because, as I was translating *Won't You Stay, Radhika?*, I was struck by how much the mood of ennui dominated the book. In Usha Priyamvada's slight novel, our heroine, Radhika, is afflicted with ennui in the truly French sense of the word. Yes, her sheer motionlessness and inaction could be interpreted as a clinical depression, but her mood lacks the heaviness or sorrow of that emotion and is reminiscent of Cécilie's strange melancholy or Emma Bovary's spidery ennui.

As I edited draft after draft, I felt Radhika's ennui dragging me down as well. 'She's still lying on the takht,'

I would write to a friend. And the next day, '...and she's back on the takht again!' And again and again, staring at the ceiling, doing nothing, caring about nothing and nobody. If, she reads a book, it does not even afford her the transient pleasures enjoyed by Emma Bovary. She avoids people, romance, family, as she lies still, or wanders listlessly through her neighbourhood. Until the distinctly unboring ending of the book, she is not inspired to take control of her life or do anything at all. And even then, it's not clear that the ennui is entirely over.

You may argue that the rasa of ennui is a luxury of the bourgeoisie, and that this emotion of the privileged is not the stuff of which great literature is made. On the first count, you'd be right, but on the second count, I would disagree. As readers we are impoverished by the narrowness of the emotions a female character is allowed to experience. The focus on hetero-normative romance in fictional heroines is a device that ultimately centres women's lives around men. This is not to say that Radhika is without love interests in the novel; after all, there are three men in her life. She does not always feel detached from these men, but ambivalence, or boredom, or ennui, is the primary lens through which she views them: these are all interesting shades of emotion for a heroine to experience, and we should welcome them.

Of course, there is also the matter of her strong attachment to her father. Could this be an 'Electra complex' as her stepmother and one of her love interests suggest? With the early death of her mother, Radhika was raised by her father. Their bond is not just emotional, but intellectual. Radhika helps her father with his art history writing and pursues a degree in the arts herself when she goes to the United States. She feels betrayed by his sudden marriage to Vidya, an emotion which sets off much of the plot. Without spoiling the story, let us simply say that this is a possible lens for viewing the book, and a feature that is shared with *Bonjour Tristesse*. But I would argue that in both cases, the Electra complex solution is overly simplistic. It should also be noted that this psychoanalytical assessment is raised by two of the more unsympathetic characters in the book.

And then there is that stint in America. Published in 1967, *Won't You Stay, Radhika?* is probably one of the earliest instances in Hindi of diaspora literature. Radhika has only been gone for a couple of years. Filled with a sense of alienation in Chicago, she longs to return to India, hoping for a sense of belonging. But the return, as has since so often been recorded, is alienating as well, leaving her in an emotional state of in-between-ness, of universal unbelonging. A sense of alienation is also famously a hallmark of Hindi literature of the 1960s, where it is usually traced to urbanization and the breakdown of traditional family structures. In Usha Priyamvada's debut novel, *Fifty-five Pillars, Red Walls*, and in Mohan Rakesh's *Andhere Band Kamre*, we see variations of this same trope playing out: an alienated twenty-something living alone in Delhi, but without the ennui.

Alienated and paralyzed, Radhika is faced with the classic dilemma of whether to stay or return. Neither option appeals, and she feels no strong pull to keep her anywhere or with anyone. She is already 'ruined' for traditional marriage, as one relationship demonstrates; she can't go back to living with her father, and yet there is nothing she particularly misses abroad. And so she lies on the takht. Bored. Melancholic. Immobile. Although the title of the novel refers to a particular scene, that question mark hovers over the entire work: What will you do Radhika? Will you get up off the takht? Will this ennui ever come to an end?

—Daisy Rockwell
2023

1

Nothing had changed. Everything was the same as it had always been, back when Radhika had known it so well. This was how she'd remembered it: Delhi dust, hazy evenings, grimy foliage, rough pavement. Radhika saw and recognized it all. There was a certain thrill in the familiarity: *Ah, everything has stayed exactly the same!* But when she dug deep, Radhika did feel a tiny sliver of disappointment: everything looked so colourless and drab. She'd grown accustomed to the sparkling brightness in Western countries without even realizing it.

Radhika turned to look at the street. There was an incessant stream of busses, bicycles, and pedestrians. But, the Indian faces looked prosperous in their own milieu. She too was one of them, a part of this crowd. She could lose herself here and no one would notice her. This long-awaited moment, her first evening home after three years abroad, was now before her. But she felt a growing sense of despair.

No, she wouldn't allow herself to be moody this evening. She glanced at Akshay in an attempt rise above her mood.

He had been standing near her all this time, silently, as though he didn't want to intrude on her thoughts.

Akshay.

He'd met her at the airport that morning. Radhika had never seen him before. She'd been rather surprised when she learned he'd come to fetch her. But she liked what she'd seen at first glance. He wore a reasonably well-tailored suit. The tie was nice too—not too flashy, nor overly sober. He had strong wrists, polished shoes, hair that was not too long. When he avoided looking directly at her, she supposed he might be shy around women, and smiled at the thought. Radhika had now left off thinking too hard, her eyes darting about as she took in the Indian sights.

When she hesitated before stepping into the restaurant, Akshay stopped as well. He was surprised, but only a little. Ever since he'd brought her from the airport that morning, he'd been periodically surprised at her behaviour. She seemed so detached from all this. Though he didn't wish it, her uniqueness was starting to impress him. All day at the office, he'd wondered what it was that made her so unusual. Strong self-confidence? A certain sophistication that arises from living and studying abroad? Or the dignity and mystique that comes from being the daughter of an unusual father? He couldn't put his finger on any one quality.

That morning, as all the passengers disembarked from the Pan Am plane, he'd somehow known the moment he'd seen her that she must be Radhika. Nonetheless, he was a bit shocked. The night before, her stepmother, Vidya, had placed a trunk call to him and urged him to meet Radhika at the airport; to look after her properly, then put her on the night train. She was returning home after years away, and Vidya was unable to come, though she wished she could.

Akshay had known Vidya a long time. His elder sister, Anjali, had been a classmate of hers. He was well aware that Vidya wasn't easily excited or shaken, so Akshay had been surprised by the urgency of her tone. He'd developed a mental image of Radhika as a shy, skittish girl who would be helpless and quick to weeping, despite returning with an MA degree from abroad. Although, what he'd learned from Vidya herself did not match this image at all.

He was still waiting outside when Radhika got off the plane and went over to the customs counter. After about three quarters of an hour, she had come out and stood on the stairs. Akshay wanted to stop for a moment and take a good look at her before approaching her. That way it would be easier to figure out how to behave.

Radhika had looked exhausted. A large suitcase stood beside her, and she held a matching pale-grey cosmetic case in her hand. She kept touching her hair to adjust her loosened bun. Akshay walked over and said hello.

'Hello, my name is Akshay. Vidya asked me...your mother sent me...she wasn't able to come herself...'

Radhika started, then greeted him with a look of curiosity.

'...she called me last night and said you were coming and that I should come to meet you,' finished Akshay.

Radhika said nothing to all this. She bit her lower lip and stared back at Akshay.

'Let's go,' he said.

Not getting any verbal response, he picked up her suitcase. It was fairly heavy. He walked towards the taxi, waiting. Radhika followed quietly. When the door was opened for her, she sat down.

He hadn't yet got the impression that Radhika was helpless or skittish. He did feel she looked sad now, or maybe she was just tired after a long journey.

'When did you leave New York?'

'Yesterday morning,' she said.

She began to stare out the window, as if there was anything visually arresting to be seen on the way from the airport to the city: Brambles lined the street, mustard flowers dotted the fields, a few well wheels turned in the distance.

'Quite a bit looks changed to you, probably,' he suggested after a long silence.

'Not really,' laughed Radhika. Her laughter didn't sound joyful. A Western custom, perhaps.

'How do you know Vidya?' she asked suddenly.

Noting that she called Vidya by her name, and not *Ma* or *Mummy*, or some other form of familiar address, Akshay told her that Vidya and his sister had been classmates.

'You've seen her recently?'

'I went over there recently—on Dussehra—I saw her then.'

'Everyone...' Radhika paused for a moment. '...everyone must be well?'

'I only saw your father briefly. These days he's writing a book about modern painting. But you must already know that. Vidya was fine. No other special news.'

'And how is everything else there?' Radhika asked.

'That, you will see for yourself,' said Akshay. He leant forward and began giving directions to the taxi driver.

Akshay had a flat in a new neighbourhood in South Delhi. A row of tall houses lined the street, facing another row on the other side. He'd already arranged for her ticket on the night train. At first, he'd thought he would put her up at a hotel, then he thought she could simply go to a hotel herself. But Vidya had appointed Akshay for this task so Radhika wouldn't have to spend her first day back alone. So, he took her to his own home. As he unloaded the luggage and paid for the taxi, Akshay worried Radhika might be inconvenienced by his simple home, after the glamour and glitz of abroad. Radhika weakly tried to pay for the taxi, but he stopped her. When he came upstairs, Radhika was standing in the sitting room.

'Please have a seat, why are you standing?'

Radhika sat down. The room was square. There was a sofa against the wall, a leather chair—clearly of the Scandinavian style—and a full bookshelf on the side. Everything was neat and tidy, but lacking in ambiance.

A servant came in with a tray, placed it on the table

and stood respectfully to one side. Radhika was surprised by his appearance. He looked Tibetan; neatly dressed, and extremely polite.

'Sonam,' Akshay said, 'this is Radhika, she's just returned from abroad.'

The servant bowed in greeting to Radhika then began to prepare the tea.

'You're being inconvenienced on my account,' said Radhika, turning to Akshay, her cup in her hand.

'No, nothing of the sort.'

He drank his tea and went to the office.

Now the house was completely still; she couldn't even hear Sonam rattling around in the kitchen. She sat silently for a while, repeating to herself that she'd come home to her own country. Today was her first day in India. But no kin had come to greet her at the airport. She sat in the home of a stranger, the sort of person who says nothing of himself without being asked. All she knew was that he had a small flat and a Tibetan servant.

She was alone.

She had imagined this day many times. She had believed that Papa would surely come to fetch her even if Vidya did not. Then the two of them would stay someplace nice and Papa would take her out to dinner. She would order the food she'd longed for while away: beautifully puffed, crispy puris; a spicy tarkari of Kabuli chana, decorated with thin slices of green chilli and lime; paneer koftas; gujiya soaked in yogurt; chutney; all types of pickle; peppery pappadums;

and for dessert, carrot halwa sprinkled with dry fruits, or freshly cut mango slices and cream, or thick syrupy kheer fragrant with saffron.

'The hot water is ready for you,' Sonam told her.

Radhika bathed and went to lie on the sofa. The room had filled with sunlight, and that pleased her. She spread out her wet hair on a cushion and covered her eyes with her arm.

She wished she could forget the terrible memories. Yes, she'd gone abroad after a horrible fight with Papa, but that had been three years ago. She'd begged forgiveness and returned. Was Papa still holding a grudge against her? If not, why hadn't he come? Fathers and children struggle in every household—but this hadn't been an inter-generational struggle. Radhika had fought for her personal freedom. It had been Papa who had taught her not to fall in line. She knew her behaviour had upset him, but she'd never imagined he could be so cruel, so hard. On her way home, she'd sent him a cable, believing he'd have forgiven her by now and would come to get her in Delhi.

She'd looked around eagerly as she got off the plane but had seen not one familiar face. The older American who had sat in the seat next to her from London to New Delhi had turned to her and smiled.

'How does it feel coming home after so long?' he'd asked.

Radhika couldn't immediately respond. She glanced once more at the row of people leaning over the railing and felt suddenly emotional. Everything here belonged to her—the dust-clogged air, the pale sky, the sun-scorched grass, the hard earth beneath her feet—she was an indivisible part of all of this. How could she express in one sentence all she felt at that moment? But the man was expecting an answer, so she laughed slightly and said, 'Just wonderful!'

Radhika began to scan the crowd again. The people hanging from the railing were waving, their arms undulating like the sea. A small clutch of girls stood to one side on the steps; an elderly couple carefully scanned the faces of the arriving passengers in an attitude of serene anticipation.

Surely a friendly face would appear the moment she cleared customs and came outside. Everyone in her family shrank from emotional displays. Maybe that's why no one had squeezed forward to throw their arms around her. But joy cannot be disguised.

Radhika arrived in the lounge with the other passengers. The customs officer was young. He sported a small moustache and his shoulders were stiff with the awareness that he was the one and only arbiter in the situation. Radhika was not offended by his taking care of the foreigners first; it was only proper, after all. As she sat on the cane sofa awaiting her turn, she felt a bit hopeless. Other people's relatives began entering to greet them in the lounge. Even the elderly couple had found their son and his white wife, and now all of them stood about, as Radhika contemplated her dreadful situation.

She wouldn't look over at the door anymore. Instead, she began glancing towards the customs counter again. When her turn came, she rose with a feeling of calm control and handed her passport and suitcase keys to the customs agent.

He read her passport, then glanced at her.

Date of birth: January 1940
Height: five feet three inches
Weight: one hundred five pounds
Profession: Student

And one more glance.

All men looked at her twice, this Radhika knew. The first time cursorily, the second, attentively. She knew the reason, but she didn't accept it. At first glance, she looked like any other Indian woman: a fair complexion, black eyes, black hair. But there was also something they saw in that first glance that made them look again.

'You were studying there?' asked the customs officer as he filled out the forms.

'Yes!' replied Radhika.

'What was your subject?'

'Fine arts.'

'Will you open your suitcase?'

'Yes, of course.'

Radhika opened her suitcase. She knew that everything she had would be opened, but she wasn't concerned. She hadn't brought a transistor, camera, or tape recorder. As the customs officer noted this on the form, he looked up at her again.

He laughed as he closed her suitcase, and asked, 'So what have you brought then?'

Radhika made no reply.

When she turned away after signing the papers, she

remembered again that once she exited, she would be returning home after three years, and that no one at all had come to greet her. How wonderful it would have been if Papa had come! But there were other people who could have come as well, such as her elder brother, Vinay, her sister-in-law, and their children, Veena and Vivek. She'd given them plenty of notice. As she wondered what she should do now, she stood by the stairs, gazing vacantly over the swarming taxis, the colourful turbans, and Air India posters. She had never contemplated the possibility that she'd have nowhere to stay after getting off the plane. Of course, her childhood friend, Prabha, did live in Delhi. But Radhika didn't feel like searching for Prabha's husband's name in the phonebook and imposing herself on them. Then what should she do? She could spend her time at the station and go home by the night train.

Home...if she had a home anywhere! Papa's home? Her elder brother's home? No one from either place had deemed it necessary to come and fetch her.

Right when she'd decided she would go directly to the station and had turned to hail a taxi, Akshay walked up quietly and stood near her.

When she heard what he had to say, Radhika felt she'd been saved. Now she wouldn't have to spend the entire day in the waiting room. She stared directly at Akshay and thought she liked him: he was serious, unassuming, and soft spoken. Since Vidya had sent him, it would be proper to accept his hospitality. And then, she had only to spend a few hours with him.

She turned over on the sofa. She felt increasingly agitated and buried her head in the pillow. When she closed her eyes, she felt as though she was still in her seat on the plane—the twinkling lights of Beirut lay below; Tehran was in a deep sleep.

She must have dozed off at some point the night before. As the first rays of the morning sun had shone on her face through the window, a deep voice echoed in her ears: '*We will be landing in New Delhi in thirty-five minutes.*'

Radhika woke fully and pressed her face against the window, her heart full of longing to see what lay below.

She wasn't embarrassed by these feelings. One day, last year, she'd suddenly decided that she should live in her own country, and ever since, she'd stuck to her plan.

Radhika dug deeper into her past. Her mind slowly returned to the things she'd left behind. She'd never expected to leave India forever. How long can anyone stay contented entirely cut off from their own life?

Back there, there had been the same blue, star-studded sky; flowers bloomed, snow melted, the reflections of buildings trembled in the waters of the lakes, and lovers roamed hand in hand at dusk. All of it was beautiful. One could never feel bored in the constant flow of life. When they were tired, they could sit on colourful chairs, sipping coffee or beer in the open courtyard of the student union in the weak sunlight of the late afternoon, listening to the music students performing jazz. Boats sailed in the lake in summer, and Radhika would often swim with the other art students in the shade of the shrubberies that grew along the shores.

The art students were open-minded at any rate, and were considered avant-garde. They had welcomed Radhika into their circle without hesitation. It was a culture where no one interfered in the personal lives of others, but all the same, they'd learned a few things about Radhika; such as that her father was a renowned art critic, that she'd not only left her country with a journalist, but had lived with him for an entire year. Things had got tense between them, and now she was trying to develop her own artistic potential.

That room on Fourth Street. When she'd arrived in the city two years before, she'd got Mrs Homer's address from the university housing authority. Her dilapidated old house was on the corner, and she had a spare room on the lower storey. Radhika had rented the room, although she fleetingly missed the thirty-third floor flat facing Lake Michigan where she'd lived the first year.

After arranging her room and moving in her things, Radhika had started to work. She helped an American professor teach Sanskrit for two or three hours every morning in the Linguistics department, and in the late afternoon, she attended classes as a student. When the weather was nice, she'd sit on the swing on Mrs Homer's veranda, staring at the street, pondering herself and others.

It was during those days that she'd started to feel horribly homesick. Home meant Papa and the days before his marriage to Vidya, when there had only been Radhika in his life. His daughter, the companion of his solitude, the axis around which his entire world revolved. He spent most of his time reading and writing. There was no room for a new wife in such a life. But Radhika had had to move aside to make room for one, something she would never forget.

During solitary moments, when she was living in Mrs Homer's house, or when she awoke suddenly at night, it seemed to Radhika that she had done Papa a great injustice. It was wrong of her to want all his attention for herself. He'd spent eighteen years alone after her mother's death. Was it really all that surprising? Radhika now knew how terrifying loneliness could be.

And then, she kept feeling that she should finish her education as quickly as possible and return to Papa. She would move back to her childhood room without quarrelling with Vidya, and once more attempt to gather the scattered pieces of her life. She had spent two years there, and now she had returned. And here it all was: the sky was as she had remembered, the fruits had the same fragrant smell, the saris dangled and fluttered outside the shops. There were Indian faces all around, but had the flame that still burned within her been extinguished all at once?

2

Radhika awoke in the morning and stared out the window of the train. Every town had looked the same since leaving the station.

She had had to depart for home by the night train. She watched the parallel train tracks as they curved off to the right in the distance. She saw the rows of railway workers' quarters, their windows opening towards the tracks, and a long-faced woman peering out from one open shutter. Layers of soot covered everything. Clouds of dust floated by, purple flowers dangled from wild vines, and lotuses blossomed in small tanks. There were toddy trees, village houses smeared with yellow mud, mango groves, and plows moving sluggishly between fields. Radhika had seen all these sights while travelling back and forth hundreds of times, but today it was thrilling, because she felt at one with this dusty earth. How dry the North-Indian earth seemed to Radhika at that moment, how flat the fields. But all this was hers—her heritage.

The train was crossing the bridge over the Ganga now.

The river flowed lazily in a slender stream between the grasses, slowing here and there among the mounds of sand. Radhika recalled how they'd always had to cross the Ganga on the way to Nani's house when she was small, and how gleefully she tossed copper coins into the water below. What a feeling of accomplishment it had been when her paisa fell below the bridge!

Akshay had brought Radhika to the station after giving her a bit of dinner at his home, because the train left at eight forty-five.

And now she listened to the hubbub of the Indian stations—our own! for the first time in so long, and none of the smells were unappealing to her: the frozen fish on ice, the fruits in various states of ripeness, the sweat and dirty clothing; even the fine layer of coal dust.

Radhika had pushed down her window so she could see the passers-by only from the waist down—anxious women in long ghaghras, feet running here and there, hands holding staffs and bundles; alarmed country folk; milkmen clanking between the empty compartments; and occasionally, fashionable people strolling back and forth in front of the compartments. How had she forgotten all this? Her thoughts were still full of the ambiance of international airports, brisk but peaceful with their soothing fluorescent lighting. Only last night, she'd been buying cognac for Papa at the airport duty-free in Beirut.

Akshay had got off the train after helping Radhika to her seat. He had stood casually resting one arm on her windowsill and the other on the next window. There were many things left to say, but silence also felt natural between the two of them. Staring at the platform, Radhika occasionally cast a glance at him, and he occasionally glanced from Radhika to the platform, when he worried she might find his staring rude. Radhika must have slept deeply during the day because her face looked calm and rested in the dim blue light of the platform.

Akshay felt a bit sad that Radhika was leaving his life so quickly, and that he wouldn't get to know her better. But she was simply waiting for the train to leave. And when it had, she'd watched him standing lost in thought at the station. For a moment, she worried she hadn't properly expressed her gratitude. Once she got home, she'd write him a letter.

She stared out at the lights of the receding station, then at the darkness punctuated by plumes of smoke from acid factories. Then a cool breeze. The plump woman on the seat across from her had fallen asleep the moment the train had started. But Radhika was wide awake in anticipation. The train began to move more quickly than before. But then, the pace seemed quicker at night. Nothing was visible through the filth-encrusted window, no cities twinkling in the darkness, nor even stars.

Would this train make no stops? It roared along through the darkness, passing one station after the next without halting, their names illegible due to the speed.

Radhika heard only the whooshing of the engine in the stillness. There was a dim blue light inside the compartment.

She walked around the closed compartment twice and then went and stood in the corridor. She was the only person awake there, the only person awake on the train in the middle of the night. Nothing was visible outside in the deep darkness, only the sparks from the friction between the wheels and the rails flashing like fireflies.

Radhika had loved trains since childhood. She could spend all night awake on one, and it wasn't yet midnight. Her thoughts felt suspended between the jolts and the shocks of the train. She began to think ahead, about tomorrow, but then she stopped herself. For the past few years, she'd felt as though she were travelling in a long dark, cold tunnel with no clear goal or endpoint.

She went inside, locked the door and laid down on the seat to wait for tomorrow. She had no idea when she fell asleep after that, and only awoke when they changed tracks. They'd reached a large station, she realized. She sat up and raised the window. The cool September breeze made her shiver. In front of the locked railway crossing gate stood a few rickshaws, some cars, an old man, a neem tree, coal and ashes. She got up and went out onto the platform. Everything looked sleepy in the light of the rising sun. Radhika must have made countless journeys on that railway line, but it had felt strange to see so many familiar sights over the course of the past night. She had stoically left all this behind and gone abroad, where, if she recalled anything from home at all, it would probably have been something about special holidays, or the changing seasons, or the flowers. But the memories of these small, unremarkable things must have remained in her subconscious, otherwise why would she be so filled with nostalgia on seeing them again?

Radhika hesitated for a moment when the bearer came to ask about tea. She recalled her doctor's advice that she should take care with what she ate and drank for a few days, and not accept anything unless she knew the cups and dishes were clean. So she turned down tea from the bearer, but when another tea seller emerged calling out 'Chai!', Radhika called him over and bought a cup for twelve new paisas.

The tea was extremely sweet and hot. She began to sip it slowly, and when it was finished, she tossed the cup out of the window. When the train stopped at Lucknow station, Radhika began yet again to search for a familiar face in the crowd. She'd have to change trains to visit Papa. Her brother, Vinay, lived here, and though she didn't want to, she might have to visit him first. He hadn't been able to come to Delhi for some reason, but he might come to meet her here, or send the children. Radhika would recognize the chauffeur.

She stared outside attentively, pushing away all the memories that suddenly flooded into her mind. Childhood, Ma, and the 9 a.m. mill whistle, the school bus, stealing tiny new mangoes, Ma's diamond nose-ring, her childhood, Vidya, Ma's departure, the parrot, Mitthu, anxiously circling his cage as he tapped at his water dish, the sharp fragrance of the ras-kheer Nani always made, soaked water chestnuts.

'Radhika?'

Her uncle, Rajju Mama, stood right by the window of her compartment.

'Radhika!' he said again. She started and greeted him with a namaste.

Radhika saw Rajju Mama's wife, Suneeti Mami, come puffing behind him with her two cheerful children.

'Namaste ji!' they both said at once and rushed to open the door. First the elder one bent over to touch her feet, then the younger.

'Oh, please, stop it!' cried Radhika, lifting them up before blessing them. She hugged them both tightly as she wondered why uttering a blessing had come so naturally to her at that moment. Giving blessings made her feel just as awkward as having her feet touched.

'Get her luggage down quickly,' Suneeti Mami told Rajju Mama.

'But wait, they must be expecting me at home,' Radhika blurted out.

Suneeti Mami gazed at her mysteriously. Rajju Mama stopped as he was climbing into the compartment. Then Suneeti Mami laughed and said, 'Oh, what difference does it make if you stay a few days? We've been waiting for you and watching the trains morning and night for three days!'

Radhika watched as her luggage was removed and then got out herself. She had felt joyful at this unexpected meeting, but now she had to admit that she had been dejected since yesterday morning when she'd realized not a single member of her family had come to meet her. She had tried to remain detached, so she wouldn't feel sad. This detachment had always been a kind of armour for Radhika: *So what if someone did something to upset me, what do I care?* The feeling had been her companion for years. Now as the two children, one small, one large, gazed up at her with smiling eyes, she felt as though that armour had been cast aside, and she again feared being injured.

The elder child stuck to her side as they climbed the stairs to the station. 'Did you forget how to speak Hindi?' he asked.

'Why would I forget?'

'I just wondered.'

Radhika then remembered her duty as a guest and began asking questions about the family: What class did they each study in? Where was Nani staying these days? And how many kittens had their piebald cat had since she'd last been there? Amidst this back and forth, Radhika got into the tonga with everyone, and they set off.

By now, it was much lighter, and there was more traffic on the street, although all the shops in Aminabad were still closed.

'Our Radhika hasn't changed a bit, I must say,' said Suneeti Mami to Rajju Mama.

Rajju Mama nodded his head in agreement and smiled as he glanced at Radhika.

Now that it was lighter outside, Radhika noticed for the first time how white Rajju Mama's hair had turned in just three years. Suneeti Mami wore a grey handloom sari, a small bindi on her forehead, and worn toe-rings on her feet. She had the hands of a hardworking housewife. But at that moment, she looked happy.

'If we hadn't come to the station, Radhika would never have gotten off here, would she?' observed Rajju Mama, with a glance at his children. 'She didn't even send us a letter to say she was coming.'

'I had so much to do before leaving, I didn't have time,' explained Radhika, feeling a bit awkward that it hadn't once occurred to her to write to Rajju Mama.

On her mother's side, Radhika had three uncles, one aunt—a child widow—and her elderly Nani. Rajju Mama's family occupied three rooms in the nine-room family house in Lucknow. Her aunt—Mausi—and Nani lived by turns with each of the uncles.

'Oh, but how is Vinay?' asked Radhika.

'He's doing well. Loads of money coming in. You'll be able to tell the moment you see his wife,' said Suneeti Mami.

'I thought he might come to the airport. But he must not have had time.'

'He's opened a new cinema here. It's called the Veena,' said Rajju Mama.

'The Veena is big now,' interjected Suneeti Mami.

The tonga was turning to the left. All of a sudden, Rajju Mama said, 'Radhika, if you want to stay with Vinay, we'll take you over there.'

Radhika saw that Suneeti Mami and the children were all looking at her.

'No, Rajju Mama, I'll go with you,' she replied casually.

Rajju Mama seemed reassured.

'Go to the office and phone to them that we've picked up Radhika,' suggested Suneeti Mami.

The tonga stopped in an old neighbourhood in front of the house that Radhika knew so well.

As they were unloading the luggage, Mausi came out wiping her hand with her palla, and hugged Radhika tightly. As she stepped away from her, Radhika noticed a small tear on her wrinkled cheek.

Suneeti Mami directed Radhika's luggage to be placed in her room.

'You go wash up now, and by the time you're done, breakfast will be ready. What will you eat?'

'Whatever's convenient for you,' said Radhika. She began looking for the key to open her suitcase.

Rajju Mama had shooed the children away, and Radhika was left alone. The room was fairly large. The walls were bare—not a single picture or calendar—save for a large, old key that hung from a nail. There were two windows, through one of which you could see a tree laden with red flowers, and through the other, a sari with a black border that hung from the clothesline. Radhika stared out the window for a while, then called to Suneeti Mami without opening her suitcase. She had been nearby and rushed in smiling.

'Mami, I need a sari—a cotton one, laundered by the dhobi, and properly starched.'

When Suneeti Mami had first come to this house as a bride, her skin glowed, her eyes sparkled, and a dimple appeared on her left cheek when she smiled. The dimple was all that remained.

'Why? There must not be many dhobis over there.'

'Over there, I was the dhobi, the cook, the water woman, everything.'

'Well then, Radhika, you must have become very adept at housework.'

Suneeti Mami brought out two saris for her. One was plain, the other was embroidered with white chikan. They looked inexpensive: the one with chikan-work had thin pink fabric, lightly decorated. Radhika chose that one.

As she bathed, Radhika thought about how out of place her foreign soap looked next to the old lota, bucket, and bathing stool, stained black from bath water. She was also a bit surprised at herself that all of this—the atmosphere around her—didn't bother her at all. It was true that signs of their lack of wealth were immediately noticeable, such as Rajju Mama's poor health, or the younger child's worn but polished shoes, or the peeling whitewash on Suneeti Mami's walls, or the patches on Mausi's sari. Everything had been like that before, more or less—a secondary school teacher only makes so much—but their suffering hadn't pained her like this. And had Suneeti Mami felt distressed by Radhika's new suitcase and matching cosmetic case, her large Italian purse and Italian sandals, and her getting out of a first class compartment? But she knew that Mami wasn't like that. She was probably happy for Radhika's prosperity.

Radhika was pleased with the spring weather once she finished with her bath. Her hair hung loose down her back, and she felt more carefree in the starched sari.

Breakfast was on the table. Carrot halwa garnished

with dried fruit, pieces of petha soaked in rasa, a couple of different types of dalmoth, fresh mathris, potato lacche, and toast, butter and jam.

'Will you take an omelette or a fried egg?' asked Rajju Mama.

'Why did you go to all this trouble? I just drink a cup of coffee in the mornings, that's it.'

'Make some coffee, quick,' ordered Rajju Mama, looking at his wife.

'No, no, leave it be,' said Radhika, 'I drink tea, too, Mami, don't trouble yourself.'

'Radhika Jiji, eat a jalebi. I just got them, they're nice and hot,' said the elder child.

Radhika picked up the jalebi and popped it in her mouth. 'They're wonderful.'

He smiled. Radhika felt like breakfast took hours. She was forced to eat each and every thing. She ate it all, and praised it all, until she felt that all her praise was becoming mechanical; but there was always something else to taste, and she did like that Suneeti Mami remembered which things she liked.

After breakfast, she lay down on the charpoy and Mausi came and sat nearby with a thali full of washed masoor dal in her hand. She began picking over the dal, an old pair of glasses balanced on her nose.

'Tell me, Mausi, how are things here? Is Nani with Bade Mama?'

'You can see for yourself how things are here. It's all

God's will. Rajju's health gets worse with each passing day and your eldest uncle is no help at all. He doesn't keep Amma with him, she ends up at middle brother's house...' Mausi left off in the middle of her sentence, and asked, 'And you, dear? You did an MA, yes?'

'Yes, I did.'

'So what's your plan now? Will you get a job, or...'

Radhika was silent a moment. 'I haven't decided anything yet, Mausi. I got so exhausted working there for two and a half years that I feel like resting for a few months now.'

'Will you stay over there, with Vidya?'

Mausi could ask all sorts of questions because she was older, even those that Radhika herself did not know the answers to.

'I'll stay if she'll have me,' said Radhika.

'Why wouldn't she? Vidya never quarrelled with you. She'll have you.' Mausi plucked out a pebble from the dal.

'Your brother turned out like this as well.'

Radhika was silent.

'Suneeti saw Veena one day in the bazaar. It was she who told her that you were coming very soon. We've been waiting ever since.'

'Veena must be very grown up by now,' said Radhika.

'She's turned out just like you. Vinay opened a cinema hall in her name.'

Mausi pushed her sliding glasses back up her nose.

That evening Rajju Mama took Radhika to Vinay's house. No one else came along. Suneeti Mami looked crestfallen. She didn't expect Vinay and his wife to let Radhika return. They were her actual brother and sister-in-law after all. The children wouldn't like it if she didn't come back so she reminded them to do their homework and kept them with her at home.

For a moment, Radhika felt awkward about getting into the rickshaw, but when Rajju Mama insisted, she sat down and they set off.

'What are you planning to do now, Radhika?' he asked.

'I don't know, Mama!'

'You should get married now,' said Rajju Mama gravely.

Radhika stared straight ahead without saying anything. Rajju Mama asked lightly, 'When you went there, he, I mean...' He hesitated to mention Dan's name, '...you didn't get married, right?'

'There was never any question. Dan certainly helped me go abroad, otherwise, how would I have known which university to apply to?' replied Radhika flatly.

Rajju Mama cleared his throat, and said, 'There were so many rumours here. We'd heard...'

'But Dan,' Radhika said, 'had a wife, and also a child.'

'But he was divorced, wasn't he?' Rajju Mama clarified, 'Your sister-in-law told Suneeti. We heard that he was divorced, and that he was quite a bit older than you, that's why your Papa was so opposed.'

Radhika knew Rajju Mama was just repeating things

he'd heard, and that he was inspired to tell her all these things for her own good.

'Dan got divorced after we left, and now he's gotten remarried.'

'Yes, that sort of thing goes on all the time over there,' remarked Rajju Mama simply. She thought fleetingly of Dan. All that had ended so very long ago.

'So, Radhika,' began Rajju Mama, resuming the conversation, 'You should look clearly at the future now. I have no right to give you advice, you're so much more capable than I am now...'

'Rajju Mama!' Radhika protested. The rickshaw turned onto a wide street.

'We used to come here when we were children,' Radhika said.

'Yes, it's lovely on this road when the amaltas are in bloom.'

'Do you remember, Rajju Mama, that time I stepped on a snake in the ruins at Dilkusha Kothi?'

They laughed together and the conversation ended there.

By the time Rajju Mama paid the driver, Radhika had opened the gate and gone inside. The portico looked like it had just been built. Pots of chrysanthemums lined the drive leading up to it—there must have been at least a hundred.

She hesitated a bit at the stillness that greeted her in the veranda. The gardener was working in the garden and recognized Rajju Mama. He greeted him and told him that Babu-ji had gone to Calcutta with his family; they'd be back in a week.

Radhika was offended. She turned and said to Mama, 'It seems I didn't arrive at an auspicious moment.'

Rajju Mama, standing in a state of confusion by the flowerpots, said, 'Well now, here's an excuse for you to stay with us.'

'We'll see,' said Radhika, walking towards the gate, 'did you send the rickshaw back?'

The rickshaw driver had not yet left, so they took the same one back. Stopping along the way, Radhika bought a few things for the children—fruits, sweets, etc, and the rest of the journey passed in silence.

'You've come back so soon!' cried Suneeti Mami, at which Radhika replied as casually she could that they hadn't seen them. She went inside to change her sari.

After returning from Vinay's home, Radhika felt strangely agitated. She was alone in the room and the evening was filled with a strange melancholy. Rajju Mama had gone to teach his pupil, and Mausi sat with her face covered, lost in her Radhaswami puja. The children were doing homework in the sitting room. Radhika went into the kitchen for a while and sat on a stool. But when she picked up the potatoes to peel them, Suneeti Mami laughed and took the knife from her hand. 'Why don't you go and rest?' she suggested.

Radhika went and sat on the charpoy. A dim bulb burned in the room. The street outside was calm. A cow mooed in back.

The next day she would go to see Papa and Vidya in the morning. But what would she say by way of apology to Papa? She kept turning the words over in her mind. The last time she'd gone there from this house, Papa had already left home early that morning.

And all this had simply been a way to take revenge on Papa. Dan had only been a means to an end.

3

Daniel Peterson had come to India as a reporter for a Chicago newspaper. In those days, he had taken a one-year leave and was living in an old mansion on Faizabad Road where he was writing a guidebook on India for foreigners, called *Bharat Darshan*. At that time, Radhika also visited the library often, or the archaeology department, to do research; that was where she'd met him. Like every student her age, Radhika had dreamt of foreign travel, but she'd made no attempt to pursue it; it was simply a daydream. But it had also seemed to her that that was the only way to rise above her intolerable situation at home. Dan had promised to help make her dream a reality, and when she was admitted to the University of Chicago, she was filled with gratitude towards him. But then, there was the problem of living expenses once she was there, as the partial scholarship she had received was only nominal.

Dan had suggested Radhika help him write his book in Chicago. He would definitely need help from an Indian once he'd gathered all his material.

Radhika had agreed to this with all sincerity. She was impressed by Dan's personality. He was probably about twenty years older than her. In India's warm climate, his skin had tanned to a bronze and his grey eyes looked especially piercing in contrast to his complexion. Radhika feared his wordless absorption when he was busy working, and when the opportunity arose, he would also ask for Radhika's help in the same serious manner.

Radhika did not tell Papa that she sometimes went to the library to work for Dan as well. She could tell that Papa wouldn't like it, without even telling him. He found foreigners annoying as it was. Radhika had invited Dan to the house a few times; then too, Papa had been distant. All the same, he was generous to the guest who had come to his country and his behaviour was reserved.

Radhika got in the habit of staying at the library until three o'clock and then going with Dan to his house to drink tea. At that time of day, the only servant at home was an elderly bearer who didn't understand a single word of English. Dan didn't know Hindi, but all the same, everything went smoothly. As they sat on the lawn on a winter's afternoon, drinking tea, Dan had told her about his wife. She hadn't cared for India. When Dan had been living in Delhi, she'd managed, but when he came to Lucknow, she simply refused to accompany him. One reason for this, Dan explained calmly, was that during a trip to Jaipur, she'd met a Hungarian, and without Dan's knowledge, she'd spent quite a bit of time with him. The Hungarian wanted to emigrate to America, and to accomplish this, he'd need an American wife. After thinking everything over, Dan and his wife were now separated. She had returned home, and when Dan returned, they'd get divorced. The child would travel back and forth between the two of them.

Radhika thought about their relationship for several days. What must it be like, a country like that, where people changed partners so easily? Wouldn't this cause heartbreak? She still couldn't even forgive Papa. When she brought this up, Dan laughed.

'That's because of your personality and background, Radhika.'

The two of them had already drunk two cups of tea each. Dan sat facing the sunlight; Radhika shaded her face with her hand to protect her eyes. She listened to Dan attentively.

'After your mother's death, your attachment to your father became a bit abnormal. If the Indian social context had allowed you to have more friends from the beginning then this wouldn't have happened. Then you'd be happy that your father had found happiness in life again.'

Radhika listened carefully to all that he said. Nobody had ever analyzed her character like this before.

'What? Did you have companions in childhood?' he asked.

'No.'

'At school?'

'Yes, there were, but just a few.'

'You were able to visit their homes?'

'You're cross-examining me.'

'No, Radhika,' laughed Dan. 'I'm trying to demonstrate that you've imprisoned yourself in a sorrow of your own making. Fine, so your father got remarried. You should come out of your comfort zone to see the world, expand your potential. With some young man...'

'I find young men so immature.'

'That's because you search for your father's intellectual maturity in them. Do you know why you're comfortable with me?'

'Why?' asked Radhika.

'Because somehow, you find a reflection of your father in me. Isn't that right?'

'Totally wrong,' objected Radhika loudly.

But over time, after many such conversations, she came to believe firmly that she should agree with what Dan said and go abroad at least once.

Back then, Vidya had been teaching night classes at the University, and she didn't return home until nine o'clock. She would get so tired after eating dinner that she couldn't stay awake for long. Radhika often stayed up late typing Papa's manuscript, and Papa paced about the room, periodically stopping to place a hand on her shoulder and watch her work. The previous year, Radhika had been enrolled in the first year of the history MA; but then she had quit. Radhika immersed herself in whatever she did, with the full knowledge that no one had ever pressured her. In the meantime, she had learnt typing. She'd also developed an interest in collecting bougainvillea in an array of colours, and she'd read quite a bit of foreign literature that she had always put off reading before. As she worked away in Papa's study at night, Radhika knew full well that Vidya was alone in her own room. She derived a small amount of pleasure from this.

She had shared this with Dan in a moment of self-analysis, and he had laughed.

'Radhika, how childish of you! As long as you keep working, your father will stay in the room, and your stepmother...'

Radhika gazed at Dan obliquely, 'Is no relationship pure to you?'

But Dan always made her think. It was Dan who had insisted that she tell Papa everything; even that she wished to work as Dan's assistant in Chicago.

Papa rarely got excited. His views on life were liberal. He had absolute faith in the full development of an individual. Because of this, Radhika wandered all about the city as she pleased. But she would never forget how he exploded when he learned of her plans. He told her many times that her foolishness and ignorance would destroy her life. Radhika couldn't bear to hear any of this. She felt so enraged and rebellious, nothing Papa said, nothing he expressed, was able to touch her. She sat digging her fingernails into the chair and muttering to herself, *There you go, now you know how I've been feeling ever since you married Vidya a year and half ago.* She kept wondering why she wasn't moved in the slightest by Papa's pain.

And in that state of feeling nothing, she quickly made a few arrangements and left home. Vidya did not say a word throughout. She was the one who accompanied her to the station. A brief goodbye, a few words, but by then Radhika had begun to think about Dan, who must be waiting for her in Athens.

From Athens, they'd gone to Rome, then London, and from there, straight to Chicago.

That day, the plane had been delayed in its descent and it circled the Chicago airport for half an hour due to congestion.

Radhika sat holding her breath, her face glued to the window, watching the countless lights twinkling below. A huge city dotted with skyscrapers, and off to the left, a bit further ahead, a lighthouse, which made Radhika realize that where the beam of light shone in the darkness, that must be Lake Michigan.

Dan had dozed off in the next seat, supremely unaffected by the view. The moment they set foot outside the plane, Radhika was greeted by a gust of wind, a truly sharp, chilly breeze, which made her shiver all over. Dan put his arm around her shoulders.

Dan had taken a new flat. His wife was still living in Washington. The flat was on the thirty-third floor and its balcony faced the lake. They would start searching for a separate place for Radhika the next day. Radhika went out onto the balcony and stared into the darkness. A sharp light shone from the lighthouse, and one could hear the periodic blare of a foghorn in the relative quiet.

Several of Dan's friends who had come to visit him were inside; she had no idea why she was avoiding them. Everything was so beautiful, so affecting, so new.

Radhika stood there a long time. But she didn't go inside. Suddenly she heard a voice speaking Hindi and started.

'So you're out here, we've been waiting for you inside!'

Radhika turned and looked. The Hindi was shuddh, and the pronunciation was flawless. Then several people came out onto the balcony all at once, and someone drew the curtain aside. Radhika was bathed in light.

Dan introduced her to everyone. Among his friends was also a tall Indian youth—the Hindi speaker—with someone who was perhaps his wife. Unable to bear his curious gaze, Radhika began looking around at the others. Dan had assigned the task of finding Radhika a room to the Indian man; his name was Manish.

Dan's friends stayed up until quite late. They'd brought food, drink and coffee with them. They didn't want Dan to spend his first evening alone when he'd just returned after so many years, and they hadn't expected Radhika. Whatever remained of them in Radhika's memory had by now disappeared. She was excited for a new chapter in her life. When Manish had eventually stopped trying to find her a room, she hadn't worried much. By then, she'd heard quite a bit about the hardships faced by non-white students and she also had a faint suspicion that Dan preferred to have her stay with him. Perhaps he had told Manish to stop looking for a separate place for her, without telling her.

But, after less than a year, Dan had told her coolly that he had another opportunity to travel east and he was thinking he'd accept it. Radhika would be free and could live as she pleased.

It took her some time to grasp this.

'It will take you a while to readjust, I know, and you'll also feel sad to part from me. But you're young and flexible, and you'll quickly overcome those feelings. I'm not rejecting you; I'm setting you free. The reason why I'm not asking you to come along with me is that you've never loved me, not even for a moment. Radhika, you were looking for your father in me, even as you came with me in order to cause your father pain. But I don't want to take your father's place. I'm my own person.' He paused, and then continued, 'And I was searching for my lost youth in you. I wanted to wash away the bitterness of my wife leaving me; but perhaps neither of us has been successful.'

Then his face softened.

'I'm grateful to you that you gave me some time from your young life. I also want to tell you that you should try to grow up and stop running away from life; grab it with both hands.'

Radhika felt as though she'd been turned to stone. She realized there was quite a bit of truth to what Dan was saying. She kept wanting to ask, *But what will become of me?* but she remained silent.

'I'll make some arrangements for you. My friends will also look after you, I won't run away from my responsibility towards you.'

Radhika did not wait for any of that. She left Dan the same way she'd left Papa's home. She had chosen to be with Dan when she left home, but that was no reason to become indebted to him. Dan had said that he was not rejecting her, and when she left his home, Radhika did not feel that she was leaving him. But she felt sad, regretful, distressed, and had to stop herself from weeping.

And Dan didn't even try to stop her. Both he and Radhika knew what was missing between them. Dan had passed many nights on the sofa in the living room, and she had often left him on the sofa to stand on the balcony.

Even when Dan teased her for being an ice princess or a marble statue, Radhika realized with pain that there was nothing more he could say.

Later, when she was living at Mrs Homer's house, Radhika would often wonder why she didn't find any men very attractive. Was Dan right that her feelings towards her father had grown into a sort of psychological condition, and that there was no man she would prefer over her father? Even when she went on a date, she returned home with a headache from the effort of conversing politely all evening.

It had been a long time now, and her feelings of bitterness towards both her father and Dan had been washed from her mind. She even felt a bit grateful to Dan. He had forced her to see the truth of her situation.

Perhaps Rajju Mama had given the proper advice from his perspective. She'd always been uninterested in being tied down by a job. She couldn't live with Papa indefinitely. But marriage? And who would accept her now? Nor did she have any desire to take the seven steps around the fire with some unknown man and become a wife.

But what about Akshay? Perhaps this was why Vidya hadn't come herself but had sent Akshay instead. Did Akshay know about her past?

4

Vidya.

Radhika had always felt uneasy around Vidya. She could not tolerate the frozen expression of supreme detachment on Vidya's face.

Vidya heard a sound and came outside. Radhika saw that detachment even now.

Shambhu was unloading the luggage. Vidya told him to put Radhika's things in her room.

'Did you meet Akshay?' she asked.

'Yes.'

Vidya wore a moong silk sari with a pashmina shawl. She was tall and thin, with a high forehead, narrowed eyes, a straight nose, and thin lips. Her hair was parted straight down the middle and styled simply. She had the poise of a professor and an aristocratic style of dressing.

Radhika stood outside on the porch on that late autumn morning. When she heard Vidya tell Shambhu to put the luggage in Radhika's room, she was a bit surprised. So there was still a place called 'Radhika's room' in the house.

It hadn't been turned into a guestroom, or a storeroom, or a study for Vidya.

Radhika looked all around her. The city had grown beyond Civil Lines, and what remained now was an uprooted wasteland. There had been quite a bit of land before all the bungalows had cropped up, where flowers had bloomed on their own, lending some colour and fragrance to the empty street which was otherwise clouded by dust, day and night. More recently, only the elderly gardener had tended to the garden. He'd planted some winter flowers in the front flower beds, and in the back, carrots, tomatoes, and various other vegetables. But now even the flower beds lay bare, the henna hedge had grown thin, and the colourful bougainvillea vines had perhaps been chewed up by water buffalo or goats. As Radhika stood there, the weight of time past overwhelmed her like the current of a swiftly flowing river. The moment she set foot on this land, her home, she felt her resolve begin to wobble, as though layer upon layer was being scraped away from her with sharp fingernails.

'Come in, Radhika,' said Vidya, as she adjusted the shawl slipping from her shoulder.

Radhika hesitated. She saw that Vidya was inviting her into the sitting room.

'Should I bring tea for you right now, or will you take it after washing up?' asked Shambhu, entering the room.

Shambhu was a new servant, so he addressed her in a formal manner.

'Bring it now,' said Radhika. She felt distracted. She

entered the sitting room with Vidya and sat down after casting a glance all around.

There was a new oil painting on the wall, and a new pewter statue in shades of dark brown and grey; from the Nepali tradition, perhaps. Otherwise, even on this morning, flooded with sunlight, there was a drabness about the room.

'Where is Papa?' asked Radhika.

Vidya leaned over and adjusted a cushion before responding. 'He's in the mansion across the Ganga,' she said.

'Alone?'

'No, Bhavani's there.'

Shambhu brought in the tea tray. Radhika suddenly found it difficult to breathe. She wondered if she should ask her next question.

'Since when?'

'It's been quite a while,' replied Vidya, straining the tea.

Radhika leaned back in her chair. She picked up the teacup and began to sip her tea slowly. Papa had inherited the mansion across the Ganga from her grandfather, Baba, with the rest of the properties. Radhika had heard that Baba had kept a tawaif in that house. He'd had the house built for her, to give her peace and quiet far from the city. After the tawaif's death, it had stood empty for some time, until Papa had started to go there in the summers, when Radhika was a child. He'd had one wing renovated and decorated nicely, which was where Radhika's room was. With her door open, she could see the long bridge across the Ganga, and often, at night, while sitting on the veranda, one could make out the lights of the train passing over the bridge as its roar pierced the silence. What must it be like now, with Papa living there alone? Mumtaz—the tawaif—whom Baba had called Tajo, lived until Papa had been a young man. She had even sent Radhika's mother studded bangles for the munh dikhai ceremony at their wedding. Once, as a child, when Radhika had asked what Mumtaz was like, Papa had replied briefly, 'Beautiful! She was quite fair; very cheerful...' and then he'd fallen silent. When she had first seen Vidya as her stepmother, Radhika had wondered if Tajo had been like her at all.

'Does Papa ever come here?'

'Very little. Bhavani takes him everything he needs.'

'Does he...' Radhika stopped and then blurted out, 'Does he know that I'm coming?'

'Bhavani came the day before yesterday, so I told him then.'

Radhika's eyes filled with tears so quickly that she was speechless. The tears welled up and rolled down her face. She had never cried in front of Vidya before. She bit her lips, quickly set down her teacup, and rushed to her room. She had only walked a short distance when she was forced to stop. Where there had once been a door, there were now floor-to-ceiling bookshelves.

She turned and went back to where Shambhu had emerged, and taking that route, walked to her own room, where she fell down on the bed. The pain that had stung, throbbed, enraged, wounded, agitated for three or four days had suddenly burst forth with a velocity before which she felt helpless.

The room was illuminated in the midday sun. Radhika still lay on the bed. At eleven o'clock, she heard a rickshaw bell outside, and then heard Vidya's voice telling Shambhu to make sure Radhika was fed properly. After that she heard Shambhu close the door and come inside humming.

Radhika felt light now, completely emptied; it was an unburdened feeling. She had only a slight headache and she felt utterly powerless.

This room of hers. As soon as Vidya had moved in, she'd upended the entire house. The heavy furniture from Ma's time, the cupboards, the beds, the tables, all were hidden away. Vidya seemed obsessed with smashing and breaking things. She knocked down walls in some places and put in new doors in others. Elsewhere, she boarded up doors and turned them into windows. She installed false ceilings below the high ceilings of the previous era. Papa's bedroom had been right next to Radhika's, so she could call out to him in case she was scared at night or needed something. Vidya had turned that room into a guest room and chose a room all the way across the house for her own. Radhika insisted that in her portion of the house, the room with the attached bath and veranda overlooking the garden stay exactly as it was. She liked white-washed walls and preferred high ceilings; the blue on them too.

Now, Radhika saw that a false ceiling had been installed in this room as well, and that the walls had been painted a pale shade of lavender. The furniture was the same: a bed of walnut wood, a vanity table and an almirah. The walls were bare, and her books weren't even on the shelves. Her suitcase had been placed in one corner of the room. Radhika unwillingly pulled herself out of bed and went to open the almirah, where she saw the clothing she'd left behind in the drawers. It looked as though no one had touched it. So many saris she'd already forgotten, the blouse styles outdated. There were sets of green bangles in the bangle boxes. When she slid her hand under the pile of saris in the drawer, she felt a string of rosary beads. She pulled it out and looked at it. When had she bought this rosary? Radhika had no recollection whatsoever. She felt around, and this time discovered her gold medal. She left the drawer open and went to sit on the bed, where she turned the medal over to examine it. That year, she'd come in first among all the students in the college BA exams. Her name was engraved on the medal. Only the faintest traces of that Radhika remained: the one who was innocent and naïve and took life so seriously. She had never expected or even imagined that she would come in first. Certainly she had written first class exams in the past, and when the exam results came out, she was to be treated to a fancy feast. Papa had promised. And he did throw her a feast, but the people who came were more curious to see his new bride, Vidya, than celebrating Radhika's success.

Ever since her return, Radhika had been retrieving

memories and examining them in every possible light. Back there, in America, she had neither this much free time, nor an environment to remind her of the past at every turn. When she'd been there, she'd kept herself busy all the time, so busy that she would find herself moving mechanically. She'd get so tired she'd fall asleep as soon as she lay down in bed at night. On days when her heart rebelled and her mind got tangled in thoughts of the past, she'd take a couple of sleeping pills. And when the naked branches of the trees shivered in the horrifying cold of winter, and there was nothing but snow all around, she'd long to lie down in some warm, summery place with her eyes closed. Of course, there was always the simple solution of taking pills after dinner to diminish the torment. But here, Radhika felt so alienated from all her connections, her background, and her emotions that she could do little else but sit. What else could she do besides sit around picking at the scabs on old wounds?

Holding the gold medal in her fist, Radhika began to relive that summer in her mind.

5

Papa had actually arranged for them to go to Mussoorie when Radhika's exam was over. He hadn't gone to Mussoorie for many years and perhaps he wouldn't have gone then if Bhabhi hadn't insisted on taking Radhika with her somewhere for the summer. She liked to say that both Papa and Vinay were so wrapped up in their own work, Radhika was growing up and no one was giving any thought to arranging her marriage. 'So many people visit the hills in the summer,' she pointed out. 'You might just meet a few good prospects.'

It was perhaps because he knew it would be pure torture for Radhika to spend the summer under Bhabhi's protection that Papa had made arrangements to go to Mussoorie himself. He owned a cottage on Camel's Back Road, which he had not visited for years. He decided to have it renovated that year, and left at the beginning of April, taking Bhavani with him. He had a book coming out and he'd be very busy with that, so Radhika would be free to spend time with her friends.

This was nothing new for Radhika. Papa had studied

law to please his father, and so his tarnished name plaque at the gate had continued to hang in front until recently, but she'd never heard that he'd enjoyed it. Baba had been among the most famous lawyers of his day and he had left behind a row of shops in the city and three or four homes in various places as evidence of his wealth. Papa had begun writing essays on literature and art during Baba's lifetime, but after the death of Radhika's mother, he had begun to spend all his time on such work. This had been the routine for years. Vinay went to study in Shimla, and Radhika had lived with Papa in the large, old bungalow in Civil Lines, surrounded by servants and ayahs. When summer came, they would go to the mansion across the Ganga, where Radhika spent her afternoons in the garden, picking unripe mangoes and falsa, and feasting on them.

Mussoorie had been crowded and Radhika had greatly enjoyed herself there. Vidya was staying in the cottage next door with her younger sister, Rama, and their elderly mother. Rama was the same age as Radhika, and because she came to Mussoorie every year, her circle of acquaintances was large. Radhika was enthusiastically invited to join them. She knew that Papa disliked any sort of interference when he was working, so he got a bit of peace in the house with Radhika always out. And of course, the old servant, Bhavani, was in the house, so he could make sure Papa got all his meals.

It was Bhavani who had complained first.

'She spends all day here and talks constantly to Sahib. He gets no work done at all.'

'Who?'

Radhika had been drinking her morning tea. She was still quite sleepy. Her arm lay limply across the cold satin of the quilt. She'd spent the whole previous day at a picnic at Kempty Falls and her feet still hurt.

'That Vidya, who else?' replied Bhavani, sweeping up the dust with his broom.

'Oh, Vidya,' Radhika laughed.

Whenever Vidya entered the room, Rama's girlfriends fell completely silent, and that silence would linger until she left. Although she was just a few years older than Rama, her personality was completely different. She spoke less, laughed less. So it was Vidya who was wasting Papa's time. Radhika laughed when she heard this, although she had noticed Papa and Vidya exchanging glances.

Some weeks later, when she returned from playing bridge all day at the home of some of Rama's acquaintances, Papa was pacing about outside on the veranda waiting for her. When Radhika saw him standing there, she was alarmed. She'd returned home after spending the entire day away. Bhavani must have whispered this to him, and now she'd get a scolding.

She stood on the veranda for a moment. Papa motioned for her to sit in a nearby chair. He left off pacing and took a few long puffs on his pipe. He was searching for the right words to say something. Radhika stared at her fingernails. She was completely prepared for an admonishment.

'Radhika, Vidya and I are going to be married next week.'

Radhika started and stared at him. It was as though a storm had just passed overhead. But there was the deep blue sky above the mountains and the huge zinnia blossoms outside the veranda. She dug her fingers into the cane of the chair to control herself, then stood up without saying a word and went to her room. She sat down for a while, then got up, removed her clothes from the almirah, and began laying them out on the bed.

In the past, whenever she'd been angry with Papa, she'd always threatened to run away from home. She threatened to go to Mausi, or to Vinay's hostel, and said she'd never ever stay with Papa ever again. She would take out her suitcase from under the almirah and started packing. Her scrub brush, hairbrush, comb and ribbon. She would close the door and once again count the coins in her small wallet. When she would finally re-emerge, Papa would always come out of the study to pick her up and hug her.

Radhika would shed a tear or two, then give in, and Papa would take her back and always give her some reward for giving in, like a new picture book or knitting wool to make into a sweater for her beloved puppy, or a promise to read a story aloud to her every night.

But that couldn't happen now. Papa wanted to marry Vidya. And even if Radhika left home, he might not stop her, because he knew she wouldn't go anywhere.

Why couldn't she go, she wondered? She'd taken the BA exam; she would definitely pass, and then she could get a job somewhere as a receptionist, or an air hostess, or a salesgirl.

She knew well how much that would wound Papa, and at that moment, that's what she wanted to do, to wound Papa deeply. Following her old habit, she first took the scrub brush from the bathroom and then began gathering things from the dressing table.

'Radhika.'

Vidya stood in the doorway.

'There's no need for you to leave home because of me,' said Vidya.

Radhika turned to face her. Vidya's face, always controlled, looked composed even now.

Radhika had a great deal to say, but her eyes welled with tears. After a moment, she turned her back to Vidya and busied herself with packing.

'Can the two of us not live together as good friends?' asked Vidya quietly.

'I don't need a friend,' replied Radhika tearfully.

'Hear me out.'

'You're wasting your time for no reason.'

Radhika wished she didn't sound upset and tearful. But she was unable to control herself. After Vidya left, she sat down on a chair and covered her face with her aanchal. Her belongings lay scattered on the bed.

She was starting to realize that nothing could ever be the same again. She simply could not imagine how marriage had even occurred to Papa. He must be at least twenty years older than Vidya, and why had Vidya agreed to it, knowing that Papa had two grown-up children?

Bhavani came and asked what she'd like for dinner. Papa had been invited to Vidya Bibi's house and the two of them had gone down together a little while ago.

'Nothing.'

But Bhavani still didn't leave.

'Are you going out somewhere?' he asked, seeing all her things laid out.

'Yes!'

'Where?'

Radhika had no answer to this. For the moment, she had only thought of going to Vinay's house. Vinay wouldn't allow this marriage to happen. She was sure of that.

'You'll catch the bus tomorrow morning,' said Bhavani.

'Yes, I'll go tomorrow,' said Radhika.

'Then why don't you go outside for a bit. I'll make your bed.'

Radhika got up and went to stand on the veranda. The street curved directly below her like a ribbon, and people moved about like tiny dolls. Only this morning, she had been a part of this carefree crowd, and now it seemed so far, like something that had occurred in another life. Lights lit up along the streets all at once below in the valley.

Radhika took a couple of deep breaths. Papa was not satisfied with simply being a father, a writer, a lawyer; this was clear to her now. He wanted greater fulfilment in life, from someone with a youthful body. This knowledge filled Radhika's heart with a deep revulsion. What had made him think of this, Radhika wondered. Had his chosen bride been of a more mature age, or more affectionate, perhaps Radhika would have accepted her. But Vidya? Vidya was taller than most women and she wrapped her saris with great care, to ensure that her shapely body would be clearly discernible. All Rama's friends had noticed this. And they had also noticed that because she had a certain amount of freedom, her clothing was expensive, but interesting. Rama had mentioned several times that her sister considered no man worthy of her.

Bhavani insisted she have a little vegetable soup though she refused to eat multiple times. It was getting colder, but she did not go inside, and stayed curled up in her chair. Bhavani gave her a shawl, which she unfolded to cover herself. She wanted Papa to find her sitting here like this when he returned later; then he'd understand how much he'd wounded her. At the same time, she also wondered why she wanted to arouse his sympathy by appearing in such a pitiable state. Why didn't she just pick up her suitcase and depart, like a proper nineteen-year-old girl? Without leaving any address. Then Papa would have to look for her.

Eventually she fell asleep where she sat. Papa must have got back fairly early, as she felt as though her eyes had closed for only a few minutes, but her whole body was stiff from sitting in the chair.

'Radhika, dear!' Papa whispered.

Radhika awoke to find that her foot had fallen asleep.

'Go inside and sleep properly. You'll catch cold out here,' he said, as he switched on the veranda light.

Radhika tried to get up, but she stumbled as she walked towards her bedroom, dragging her leg.

Papa accompanied her to the room and sat down.

'I want you to learn how to behave politely towards Vidya. The two of you will have to live together now.'

Radhika glanced up at him with injured eyes. It used to be that when she heard Papa's voice in the darkness, she felt he understood her well. His tone now put that delusion to rest and his words shook her life like an earthquake.

'I won't live with you people now,' she retorted.

Papa stared at her, then stood up and replied in a very measured tone, 'I hope you don't do anything in haste.'

He closed the door behind him, and she listened as his footsteps receded.

6

Vinay and Bhabhi had different reactions. Bhabhi, who had always feared that Papa or Radhika might move in with them, was perhaps even reassured. Vinay had heard the news, but he didn't know anything about Vidya. He was so wrapped up in his in-laws' business that he didn't want to get involved. With this in mind, he advised Radhika that she should go back and live at home like a good girl. He didn't like Papa getting married at this age, but he didn't wish to sternly oppose it. After staying with them a few days, Radhika noticed that Bhabhi brought up the idea that Radhika should just go back and live with Papa as much as possible.

In the midst of all this, Radhika's exam results came out, and, as hoped, she had passed in first class. This made no impression on Vinay's household, but a congratulatory telegram did come that evening, from Vidya. And only a few days later, a parcel arrived as well, containing a sari. Radhika opened the parcel but didn't take out the sari, even though Bhabhi had been searching for just such a sari for several days.

'What will you do now?' Vinay asked one day when they were sitting out on the lawn.

Vinay's mansion had been built recently, so when they sat on the lawn, they always faced the house so they could admire it. He had ordered the turf for the lawn from an agricultural institute that imported grass from New York. And it really was amazing. A vast, soft, leafy-green carpet.

After a trip abroad, Vinay had taken to drinking scotch every evening. He was on his second round at this moment. Bhabhi wasn't there.

'I haven't thought about it yet,' said Radhika.

'Your Bhabhi thinks you should get married. I think I'll write to Papa about it.'

Radhika said nothing. She continued to stare silently at the walls of the house.

'The problem is that all these things take time. It's not good for you to sit about idle until then.'

Radhika had stopped listening to what he was saying. Her glass of orange squash had long since been finished. Vinay's face usually turned red when he drank, and he had to wipe the sweat from his forehead repeatedly with a handkerchief. Sometimes Vinay seemed quite similar to Papa, Radhika thought, but his face lacked the refinement of Papa's, the result of living a life of comfort. He'd gotten married as soon as he'd left his engineering college. He now had two grown children, Veena and Vivek. Bhabhi was her father's only child, and Vinay had taken over his father-in-law's business immediately after getting married. Two mills, one sugar factory, trucks, a cinema house, and who knows what else. Papa had not arranged Vinay's marriage either. Vinay had suddenly announced that there was a girl he liked, and that he wanted to get married right away. When Papa took Radhika to participate in the wedding, Radhika kept looking at Bhabhi, and wondering what it had been about her that had made Vinay like her. It wasn't that there was anything wrong with the way she looked or sounded, but Radhika could not stand the smugness with which she kept bringing up the wealth she enjoyed due to being her father's only daughter.

Papa wrote several times to Vinay that Radhika should come home now. If she was going to keep studying at the University, she should decide on the topic and so forth. There would only be problems if she delayed. Since the letters were written to Vinay, Radhika did not reply to them.

On his return from Mussoorie, Papa stayed for some time at Vinay's with Vidya.

Radhika derived a deep satisfaction from seeing how Vinay became a bit bashful in front of Vidya. Bhabhi was in a temper. Vidya appeared totally unimpressed by all her grandeur. Moreover, she'd probably never imagined a peer for a mother-in-law, and on top of that, one who was serenely beautiful; radiant as a gleaming lamp.

When Papa wasn't directly in front of her, Radhika tried to search his face for signs that he was truly happy. She could see no change: there was the same wide forehead, the eyes blazing with brilliance below thick brows, countless tiny wrinkles. This was the same familiar face lost in thought, and whenever he smiled, his whole face lit up.

One evening, they had been all sitting on the lawn, except for Radhika, whom Bhabhi had sent a servant to fetch. She rose somewhat irritably. She liked lying in the dark air-conditioned room, and she did not want to be around Papa and Vidya either.

She came out and sat on a chair set a bit apart. She'd been wearing a pale organdie sari since morning, which was rather wrinkled by now. Vidya and Bhabhi were both dressed up, each according to her own standard. Vidya wore a white chikan sari and a loose bun; Bhabhi had put on a bit too much make-up.

'We were talking about your wedding,' said Bhabhi.

Radhika turned to stare at her when she heard this.

'She...' Vinay meant Vidya. He stopped, in a quandary as to how to address his father's wife. 'She says that you might not be happy with a hastily arranged wedding, because... because...' Vinay stopped.

'It's often the case that girls afflicted with an Electra complex aren't happy once they get married,' Vidya explained carefully.

Radhika was instantly livid, but she said nothing. Then her gaze met Papa's. He looked serious, but his eyes were filled with compassion. The two of them had always shared a silent language before, in which their thoughts were on the same wavelength. But now Papa was not tuned in; he was far away, separate from everyone, absorbed in himself.

'I don't want to get married right now,' said Radhika firmly.

Vidya and Bhabhi exchanged meaningful glances.

Then Papa cleared his throat. 'Radhika,' he said. 'I want you to come home with us.'

Radhika was outraged.

'Why do you always get what you want? Do I not have wishes of my own? I'm your daughter. Fine. But I'm grown up now and I'll do what I want.'

Papa was startled, and then he looked bitter. Radhika had never talked back to him like this.

'Radhika,' warned Vinay.

'Enough. You've never given any thought to my happiness compared to your own desires. Why don't you all just leave me alone!'

Radhika rose angrily and left. Her cheeks felt hot from the rush of emotion. She threw off her clothes and went to stand under the cool spray of the shower, but even then the heat of her anger did not dissipate.

In the end, she did return to Papa's house. Vidya herself wrote her a letter inviting her, and since Bhabhi was fairly distraught, Radhika had no choice.

7

It wasn't that the mansion was difficult to reach, or that Radhika didn't want to go; but it still took her two or three days to make up her mind to visit Papa. And in the meantime, an endless succession of visitors forced her to fulfil social responsibilities, though she had absolutely no desire to do so. Shambhu must have grown weary of serving tea and snacks. Vidya appeared infrequently, only emerging if she knew the visitors well. They were mostly Radhika's former classmates, people from the neighbourhood, and distant relations. Radhika found visiting with the latter tedious. An aunt by marriage came with her daughters-in-law and grandchildren, and stayed the entire day. She kept asking Radhika about food prices over there. And had Radhika started smoking cigarettes and drinking alcohol, and do the people there eat the same rubbishy red wheat that we do? Or do they keep the good stuff for themselves and send the rotten stuff over here? In the late afternoon, after the children had dozed off, she slid over to ask Radhika, 'Now do tell me, Radhika, after living with that man for so long, how did you keep from having children?' And then her husband, seeing his chance, asked greedily if there were really such clubs over there where men swapped wives for the weekend.

After the aunt had left, Radhika swallowed two tablets of Bufferin to alleviate her tension headache, and decided that no matter what, she would go to see Papa the next morning. At dinner, she also asked Vidya if there was anything special she wanted to send to Papa. Vidya had said nothing at the time, but when Radhika got up in the morning, she found that Vidya had not only called for a scooter rickshaw herself, but was planning to come along.

Radhika briefly considered feigning a headache as an excuse to stay back again. She didn't want Vidya to be there. But she quickly recovered from her escapist anxiety and walked out to the scooter with great self-control. It was an autumnal dawn: the sun dappled the branches of the poinsettia and the tiny harsingar fluttered in the light breeze. A few remaining blossoms fell with every puff. Two water buffalos ambled by. One stopped and casually butted against the oleander tree a couple of times before moving on. This was the first time Radhika was leaving the house since her arrival. She felt a sense of sweet surprise at all the familiar sights: the row of Ashoka trees, the sindoor-painted Hanuman beneath the peepal tree, the bathers returning lazily from their morning dip, the familiar names on the houses. When they even encountered a pair of camels along the way, she made a wish—as she used to do in her school days—that her meeting with Papa would go well. Then she laughed at herself: really, what could the poor camels do to fulfil her wishes? But her belief was still fixed in her mind, like tying a torn bit of sari in a temple or hanging a thread on the tomb of a Pir.

The scooter had just turned inside the gate when Radhika saw that Papa was strolling about in front of the house. He looked over at them and stopped. Radhika told the driver to stop, and jumped out before the scooter came to a complete stop, though she knew Vidya was staring at her strangely.

Papa remained where he was. When Radhika reached to greet him, she looked him in the face, and was shocked by how much weaker and older he looked. His hair had gone almost completely white, there were black circles under his eyes, and his face wore an air of fatigue, even on this fresh morning.

'Were you ill?' Radhika spoke first.

'No.' he paused. 'You had no trouble getting here?'

His voice, distant and formal, sent a shiver of despair through Radhika's entire body. 'No, what trouble could there be?' she responded, trying to sound cheerful.

By then, Vidya had sent the scooter driver away and walked over to them. Papa turned to face her, and said, 'Go ahead and arrange for breakfast. Bhavani must be inside.'

Vidya went inside without saying a word.

There was an old bamboo chair on the porch.

'Sit,' said Papa.

'Oh no, you sit, please,' Radhika replied.

Just then, Bhavani appeared with another chair.

'Namaste, Bhavani.'

'May you live long, bitiya. I was going to come into the city myself today. It's good you came here instead.'

Bhavani set the chair down, wiped it off with a rag, and stood close by with a look of delight on his face.

'Are you well, Bhavani?'

'Yes, bitiya. Are you well? You're thinner than you were before!'

'I'm exactly the same,' said Radhika looking back at Papa. 'But are you not taking proper care of Papa? He's grown so thin.'

The smile vanished from Bhavani's face. He sighed deeply and muttered, 'Arre, bitiya...' as he turned and left.

Papa sat impassively throughout this exchange. Occasionally, he held out his hand to examine his fingernails. The silence between them shivered at the whistle of a far-off train, and then stilled.

The desolation here was ten times greater than that at the house in the city. There had been a dense orchard of mangoes, jackfruit, sweet lime, and custard apple trees all around the house before. Radhika could tell right away that all the trees had been cut down. Only a few Eucalypti stood in front. She could tell that the house hadn't been painted for ten or more years. And this year, there was absolutely no water in the Ganga, so, only a vast expanse of sand and a bit of river grass that had grown along the banks.

Radhika sat quietly, her jaw clenched, to stop the tears that had begun to gather inside her.

'Tea,' announced Bhavani coming out onto the veranda. Papa rose first.

'Come,' he said to Radhika.

'You go in; I'll be there soon,' Radhika murmured. She wanted to sit quietly for a moment so that she could collect her thoughts and still the churn of her feelings. Once she had controlled herself like Papa, she could put on a mask and sit at the tea table.

She was forced to get up when Bhavani called out to her again a little while later. Papa still lived in the same wing of the house, but perhaps in only two rooms, because when Radhika slipped into her childhood room, she felt as though she was at a dak bungalow. It was that same type of room: impersonal and lacking in atmosphere. There was a metal bed frame in the middle of the room with no mattress, an old style of Adirondack chair, and a dusty calendar on the wall from two years ago. The only sign of life was a fresh pot of water on the stand, with a clean chillum and towels. She washed her hands and let some water drip from her fingers. *Papa probably didn't expect me to come*, Radhika thought. That's why he hadn't even had the room swept.

~

There was a round table on the small glassed-in veranda where Papa usually worked at night. At mealtimes, it became the dining table. The fragrance of fresh coffee wafted onto the veranda, and the border of Vidya's sari was visible through the open door where she stood holding a ladle.

'Bhavani, call to Sahib, so his breakfast doesn't go cold,' said Vidya. She sounded cheerful. Papa came and sat down. Bhavani set out the breakfast and pushed a plate of fruit towards Radhika.

'Eat,' he said. 'You'll get quite a bit here.'

When Bhavani brought in a plate of fried sausage and eggs, Papa glanced towards the kitchen, and called, 'You come too, Vidya.'

'Coming!'

Vidya came and sat down. So it was she who had been frying the sausages that Papa liked to have for breakfast.

'You're not eating anything?' Papa asked Radhika.

'I only take coffee and toast in the mornings, and we had breakfast right before we left.'

The sunlight fell across Papa's face, making his right temple look whiter, though most his face remained in shadow. Papa's lips had a cruel cast to them, and his chin was stern. Radhika had inherited both these traits from Papa, but her brow and eyes were her mother's. Radhika remembered her mother's shining black eyes that were even more alert during her illness—they were lively; mirrors for all her different emotions.

'You'll stay now?' asked Papa.

'No, I'm leaving tomorrow,' Radhika blurted out.

'Where do you need to go?'

'Back to Delhi.'

After that, no one spoke. The only sound was that of Vidya quietly stirring her coffee. Bhavani poured more coffee into Radhika's cup.

'Do you have something to do?' Papa asked in a subdued tone.

'I'm thinking I'll look for work. There's no point in sitting at home idly.'

Radhika picked up the cup and glanced at Papa as she touched it to her lips. Did she have any awareness of what was in her subconscious now? She hoped Papa would perhaps tell her to stay when he heard she was leaving. Maybe he'd say that Radhika should stay with him and help him. She also thought it would be pleasant to stay here alone. But Papa said, 'Whatever you think is best. You know best now.' He pulled out his chair and stood up.

8

As he entered the restaurant, Akshay thought he must be mistaken. Just four or five days before, he'd helped Radhika board the train home. How could she be here! This young woman, sitting in a dark corner, must be someone else. But when he drew near, he was quite certain. It was indeed Radhika. He had no idea when she'd returned, and if he hadn't noticed her, he might not have known for some time that she was in Delhi. Akshay walked towards her, but then stopped himself. Radhika knew his name, his address, everything. If she had wanted, she could have informed him she was coming. It was perfectly possible she hadn't considered it at all necessary to let him know.

Akshay sat down at an empty table. He could see the left side of her face and a bit of her back from where he was sitting. She wore a dark red sari and her arm glowed below her palla.

Akshay ordered an espresso and tapped lightly on the table. He kept glancing over at Radhika's table. It occurred to him she might be waiting for someone, and this made him sit up straighter, in a posture of alertness, to see who it was.

Akshay often thought of Radhika these days. He'd now reached the stage of bachelorhood when the constant flow of proposals begins to peter out. He had no complaints; in fact, he felt quite calm about it. The girls that were suggested for him were quite ordinary due to his general familial circumstances. His elder sister, Anjali, had a hand in that as well, because if he found a suitable girl, she was more concerned with her own social advancement than the salvation of a poor penniless girl.

But Akshay hadn't wanted to get married until his position in the foreign company was firmer, and now that that was the case, he considered it less of a priority.

When he'd received Vidya's call, he'd wondered for an instant if she might be up to some matchmaking. But then he'd laughed at himself. Why would a girl who'd gone off with a foreign journalist against her parents' wishes care for an ordinary man like Akshay? And Vidya was quite familiar with Akshay's views. She and Anjali had wanted to arrange his marriage with a divorced woman, but Akshay had said that though he acknowledged that the girl was a victim of circumstances, and he sympathized, he could not accept another man's leftovers. And then there was Radhika...but he'd liked the time he'd spent with Radhika after he had gone to meet her at the airport. She was not conventionally beautiful, but she was attractive. She had the sharp-witted, unaffected manner of an intelligent woman, and she exuded great self-confidence...

Akshay stood up and walked over to her.

'When did you get back?' he asked.

'This morning.' Radhika smiled slightly.

'Would you like coffee, or something else?' he asked

'Okay,' said Radhika, 'I'll have something to keep you company.'

Akshay pulled out a chair for her and sat down himself.

The coffee came out.

'I've been back in India less than a week, and I'm already wondering if I returned for no good reason,' she said, stirring her coffee.

'I've never been abroad, but I've heard people usually feel that way when they return,' remarked Akshay.

Radhika smiled.

'Where are you staying?'

'At the railway retiring room.'

'What?' Akshay blurted out.

'Yes,' said Radhika, 'I had thought I'd search for a place all day today, but I got so tired, I just slept...and now, tomorrow...'

Akshay guessed correctly what the matter was by the way she left her sentence unfinished.

'Look, I don't want to interfere in your personal life, but you can't stay on at the retiring room. You've seen my flat; why don't you stay there until you find a place?'

'But what about you?'

Radhika was impressed by his firmness.

'I'll stay in the barsati on the roof until then. I'll tell Sonam to call for his sister, Deki; she can stay with you.'

Radhika agreed immediately. She'd left home without any sort of plan, believing she could live some months off of her savings. When she arrived, she called the YWCA to see if there were any free rooms. Then she bought all the Sunday editions of the newspapers and jotted down the phone numbers for vacant rental homes. She even called several places, with no success. In the evening, she walked over to Connaught Place to avoid dejection. But as she drank her coffee, she kept feeling she'd been wrong to return to India. It would have been better to start a PhD after the MA; then perhaps she could have found a job over there. The sense of attachment that had drawn her to India and her family, had left a bitter taste in her mouth in less than a week.

Running into Akshay at this juncture had brightened her mood. But she didn't want to talk about herself, nor was she curious to learn more about him; so she thought it best to just ask about Sonam and Deki.

'My boss is from Europe,' Akshay explained. 'When they came to India, his wife took a great interest in Tibetans. She even ran a school where she gave them job training. Sonam was her cook, but now that she's gone back for a year, I've taken him on. Deki is his younger sister; she was studying in Darjeeling, but she left after finishing high school, and now she runs a crafts centre for Tibetan women. But she wants to become a doctor.'

'And your firm...?'

'It's concerned with setting up light industries in India. We get materials from abroad at very low prices, and I...I'm a planning officer.'

The waiter had come and asked Radhika if she wanted to order anything else. When she said no, Akshay paid the bill and the two of them left together. They stood for a while in front of the restaurant. Radhika was in something of a quandary, and Akshay was waiting for her to say something. Although it was getting dark, it wasn't that cold, and everything was bustling. Akshay noticed Radhika looked rather forlorn.

'Vidya is well?' he asked.

'Yes—listen, do you know of any empty flats?'

Radhika didn't wish to speak about Vidya, Akshay noted, and then he understood why she'd returned. Perhaps something had gone wrong at home again. Akshay knew Vidya's views, and no matter how much progress India had made, the social milieu hadn't changed all that much. It would take another half century for it to do so. People must still be whispering behind Radhika's back.

He was trying to understand Radhika: despite the fact that her appearance and style of dressing were completely Indian, she was not bound by tradition. Her modesty was born of humility, but not because an Indian woman should be this way. There was no trace of artifice in her. All these things were attractive to Akshay. For him, marriage must be based on mutual attraction, but what it was for Radhika, he didn't know. And Radhika was more sophisticated than he was, of this Akshay was painfully aware.

Radhika repeated the question.

'My friend Shankar lives close by; he's rented out his

two-room flat to an American Fulbrighter, but she's about to leave, so I'll talk to him. First, let's get your luggage.'

Radhika then peppered him with questions: where was the flat, how big was it, how long would it be vacant, how much would he ask for rent, was it near the market, and so on.

Akshay explained everything patiently: 'I'll show it to you tomorrow. You can pay whatever rent is appropriate. It's right near my flat. You can discuss the market and everything with Sonam.'

Radhika glanced gratefully at Akshay. 'You've solved a huge problem for me.'

That night, as she was falling asleep at Akshay's house, she thought about him. She found the two men in her family, Papa and Vinay, deeply individualistic, and to some extent selfish and ambitious. They respected women and gave them freedom as well, but only so long as they didn't cross the boundaries drawn by the men. There was also a different sort of man who considered women merely sex objects and steered clear of intelligent women. And then there was Akshay, whose generosity and nobility had impressed Radhika. Akshay would never stoop to pettiness; Radhika knew this. When they reached his home, Akshay found that Sonam had gone out for the night. He took out a clean sheet from the almirah and handed it to Radhika. Then he picked up his own bedding and went upstairs.

Radhika locked the door from the inside and began to read a newspaper before going to sleep. Akshay could tell that Radhika was still awake; the light from the bedroom below still shone.

9

What would Radhika do now, he wondered. On occasion, Akshay even felt annoyed that he was getting involved with her. He'd gone to meet her at the airport because Vidya had asked him to, but beyond that his responsibility had ended, hadn't it? No, Radhika could do whatever she wished. He would only maintain as much connection with her as was necessary within the bounds of civility.

The next day he took Radhika to Shankar's. He phoned ahead first. Shankar objected, saying he wanted to keep the rooms to himself after the Fulbright girl left, but Akshay pointed out that because Radhika had no place to stay, he himself was now homeless. When he learned this, Shankar had said, 'Okay, bring her by in the evening.'

'This is Radhika,' said Akshay. 'She returned from abroad a week ago with a degree in fine arts.'

Both of Shankar's daughters seemed impressed, and Shankar's wife, whom Akshay casually called by her first name, Prema, was warm in her welcome. But Radhika was eager to see the upstairs rooms, so she spoke little during tea, instead watching the others. Anila must have been twenty or twenty-one; she'd finished her BA and with it, her education. She often stared sweetly at Akshay, but he seemed completely unaware of this. Radhika smiled slightly when she realized this. Nina was rather attractive. She wore a chocolate-coloured churidar and a white kurta with a chocolate print. Both girls were heavily made-up for their age. Prema was also dressed up: she wore a watermelon nylon sari and a sleeveless blouse, despite the cold. Akshay noticed that Radhika looked rather plain before these three, but not ordinary.

'How are you liking India now that you're back?' asked Shankar.

'I'm enjoying it,' Radhika replied softly.

'I didn't like your country, that is, America. I went there in '56,' said Shankar, watching for Radhika's reaction.

'It's not my country,' Radhika remarked lightly.

'All the same, you've lived there; studied there,' Shankar joked. 'And perhaps you've come to adopt many Western ideals. After all, how many girls think of living apart from their parents?'

'On the other hand, how many girls' characters can fully develop here?' retorted Radhika. 'Parents constantly force their own ideas on them. As for me, I've become so accustomed to living independently, I find interference intolerable.'

'Then what will you do after you get married?' asked Prema.

'I haven't any such plans yet,' Radhika responded firmly.

'Meaning, you prefer the single life, like our Akshay,' laughed Shankar. 'We are hoping to persuade Akshay to become our son-in-law.'

Radhika understood that in his own way, Shankar was trying to tell her they had first dibs.

'Are you going to show her the upstairs now, or just keep talking?' Akshay asked, to keep the conversation from going any further. Shankar usually spoke this way, but Akshay was happy that he had never clearly spoken up about Anila, otherwise their friendship might come to an end if he refused.

Marsha Miller's things were scattered about the upstairs flat, but even amidst the disorder that occurs before one has packed and moved out, Radhika noted that the rooms had the potential to be decorated interestingly.

There were two rooms inside: one was large and square, with two windows opening onto the inner courtyard; the other was a long thin room, with windows that looked out at the greenery of far-off fields. There was also an attached bath. There was a small veranda with lattice work along the front of the rooms, and a nice wide-open roof as well.

Radhika stood leaning against the parapet for a while. All the houses in this row were the same: two storeys, connected roofs, a bit of yard in front, and beyond that, the street. On the other side of the street stood a row of houses of the exact same type. Over there, she could see a sardar seated on his own balcony, covering a child with a quilt, and a woman walking down the stairs. A little farther down the row, a young woman wearing no orhni wandered about the roof brushing her teeth, and on the next roof over, a young man watered flowers as an excuse to watch her. Radhika laughed. So the days of rooftop romances were not over. She turned and glanced to the rear: there was a dirty lane where several fat, young cows lay sprawled about ruminating with their eyes closed. Behind them stood a row of shorter houses made of brick and painted white. An unholy din rose from that general direction. In front of these houses, a milkman and a dhobi ironed clothing.

'Those people have been given notice time and again,' noted Shankar apologetically. 'We're all in favour of tearing down those huts, but so far, no definite action has been taken.'

'I'll want to come back and look again in the evening, if they don't object,' Radhika said to Akshay.

'Why would we object?' asked Shankar. It was clear that he was a bit surprised at Radhika's manner.

'Is it just as noisy here at night?'

'Noisy?' asked Prema. 'We find this lively. We dislike lonely, deserted places.'

'I'll come back,' said Radhika, walking straight downstairs.

Sonam was preparing lunch at Akshay's.

'I liked the house,' said Radhika, 'but it's very densely settled there. I've always lived in quiet since I was a child...'

'Well, you can think about what's best for you. But it's getting very hard to find places in Delhi,' said Akshay. By then Sonam had brought out a tray with two glasses of sharbat.

'All the same, a place where it's completely quiet, where not even a leaf crackles, where a whole day can pass by without seeing another face...'

Radhika was serious when she said this, but she laughed when Akshay asked, 'So what's made you so impatient for a forest retreat?'

After lunch, they went over to the sofa, and when Sonam had brought the coffee, Radhika remarked, 'Sonam, you made the coffee very well.'

He smiled, bowed, and left.

After that, the two of them sat together in peaceful silence. Akshay rose and turned the radio on low. Soft Western music filled the room.

Radhika leaned back against the sofa. Her dry, limp hair framed her face, which Akshay noted was dark brown. The hairstyle suited her, and Akshay noticed that Radhika looked good in whatever she wore. Perhaps that was how she chose her clothing. When Radhika was serious, one could clearly glimpse her father in her face.

'You weren't surprised I came back so soon?'

'No!' replied Akshay.

'Why?' Radhika was surprised.

'Because I've known Vidya for many years,' Akshay said simply.

Radhika had often read and heard that when one tells sob stories to someone completely unfamiliar, one's burden is eased. Akshay was indeed unfamiliar to her. Since Papa had chosen his own life path, why couldn't she free herself and be detached and find hers.

Her eyes rested once again on Akshay. From what she'd got to know of him during this brief acquaintance, it was clear that he would never be a lover that stirred her with excitement; his touch would never send her pulse racing. But the two of them could become friends, and Radhika did very much need an intelligent and thoughtful friend.

Radhika laughed at the pace of her thoughts, but was a bit irritated with herself as well. What had happened to her? Was she searching for the path Rajju Mama had suggested: Marriage, a household, and children? Was this all her wandering would amount to?

'I think I'll take the flat,' Radhika blurted out, rebelling against her thoughts.

10

Radhika didn't have to make too much effort in readying her home, as Marsha sold a bunch of her used things to her at a reduced price. Prema contributed some items as well, and the rest was from Akshay. Since Akshay always had lunch out, Sonam was free during the day. The three of them came to an agreement whereby Sonam could work for Radhika as needed.

Sonam and Radhika busied themselves with cleaning for two days. Then they rearranged everything several times. Since the room was square, it looked nice in any arrangement.

When Akshay came to see her in the evening, she was standing on a stool hanging a picture, her dry hair tied back in a bun, her sari palla stuffed in at the waist.

'Please come in,' she said.

'You've fixed everything up quickly,' Akshay said, looking all around.

'There wasn't much to do.'

Radhika stepped down from the stool, then stood back a bit to examine whether the picture was hung straight or not. It was a print of brilliant-yellow sunflowers; the yellow glistened, lending radiance to the room. On the other wall, she'd hung a flying bird with copper wings and a wooden body. Below, on the glass table, she had placed two small shapes. Akshay leaned over to pick them up.

'Did you make these?' he asked.

'No, I bought those from an artist from Rhode Island. He called them "hugachi", meaning, "small nothings". She took a hugachi from Akshay's hand and placed it in her palm.

'This is cast in pewter,' she said. 'Look at the form. It's a beautiful example of abstract art.' She blushed and placed the hugachi on the table.

'Sonam-la, bring Sahib some tea,' Radhika called out rather loudly.

At that moment, Akshay had a strange sensation: as though this hadn't just happened today; that he'd been waiting for the moment to come when he would return from the office and Radhika would be busy with interior decoration. And here was Sonam coming in with the tea tray. Akshay cast a cursory glance at Radhika, who still stood with her back to the window, staring abstractedly at the sunflower picture.

'Now home seems like home,' she said, glancing towards Akshay. In the buttery glow of the room, the lines in Radhika's face seemed to melt into sweetness, and her sari, though old, looked lovely on her tall, slender form.

In a moment of weakness, Akshay decided that he wouldn't fight himself this time. In the past, Akshay had suppressed his feelings whenever a young woman had come into his life. Now, at thirty, he was surprised to realize that he'd never been in love. Certainly, he'd been attracted to some women, but he'd nipped that feeling in the bud every time, before it had the chance to flower. Perhaps this was why people complained about him, and why Anila also reproached him; he knew that if he ever found peace and wanted to take Anila in his arms, she would be naturally drawn to him. The very next day, she'd say, 'Why don't you speak to Daddy about it!' He did want to be attached to someone, he wanted to let go just once and immerse himself in such an experience, but his bashfulness kept getting in the way.

Fine, he thought, *I'm attracted to Radhika for all the qualities I wouldn't want in my own wife. My wife will live in my home, she'll look after me and the children, and she'll bask in my glow. Radhika is independent, she's brilliant, but in a certain sense, she's already been married to another man...*

All the same he liked her. This time, he would not suppress his feelings. If he should get carried away in the tide, he would not thrash about to save himself.

Sonam brought in the tea. There wasn't a separate space in the flat for the kitchen, so the smaller of the two rooms had been turned into a combination storage room and kitchen. There was a takht in the front room and two chairs; Radhika's bedding would be laid out on the takht at night.

'You won't have any trouble?' asked Akshay.

'Why would I?' asked Radhika, sitting on the corner of the takht. 'And anyway, these arrangements are hardly forever.'

She held out a teacup to Akshay.

The tea was served with salty sweet biscuits.

'It's a very light tea. You must be hungry after your day at work,' said Radhika.

'Starting tomorrow, you can drink tea from my house. I'll tell Sonam. And when I get home, I'm usually...' Akshay stopped and then, feeling embarrassed, asked, 'Anila and Nina must be coming over?'

'Here? I haven't been able to invite them up since I came. Let's invite them now.'

'All right,' said Akshay with surprise. He went out of the room and leaned over the parapet to call out to Nina.

Prema came out into courtyard. She looked surprised when she saw Akshay standing upstairs. Unable to mask her astonishment, she blurted out, 'Oh, so now you've started sneaking upstairs!'

'If I were sneaking, why would I be calling down to you? Can you please send Nina and Anila upstairs?' Akshay was peeved at Prema's rudeness. Radhika had heard this conversation sitting inside. She went suddenly cold at the callous reminder that people would be offended to see Akshay visiting her frequently. This was not a country where friendship between two unmarried people could be accepted easily.

Just then, Anila and Nina arrived, talking and laughing loudly.

'Come in,' said Radhika. She stood up and went inside to get the cups herself, instead of asking Sonam to do it.

After she'd told him to put on more water and brought out the cups, Nina said, 'How beautifully you've decorated! That Marsha Miller left this place looking like a dump.'

'Who made these?' she asked, when she saw the prints hanging on the wall.

'The name is written on it,' said Anila. 'Why don't you read it?' She glanced over at Akshay and smiled.

It occurred to Radhika that she'd like Anila much more if she didn't dress up so much. Anila wore her hair in a very large bun today. She was dressed in an embroidered sari, and wore lipstick, powder, eyeliner, and strong perfume. *Am I becoming rigid and narrow-minded?* Radhika wondered. *Anila and I are the same age, so why does all this annoy me? When we start looking at our juniors with a critical eye, we must realize we are getting old, and that we're no longer flexible in our ideas.*

'What do you do all day, Anila?' Radhika asked.

'Oh, I just go to my Western cooking class, and in the evenings, I take a walk. Sometimes I read something.'

'Anila is waiting to get married,' said Nina. Then she asked Radhika, 'Okay, tell me this, you must have seen Connie Frances and Cliff Richard over there?'

In response to Radhika's questioning glance, Nina explained, 'They're singers. They must be on television.'

'There wasn't a television in our flat, so whenever I needed to see a programme, I'd go watch it in the student common room.'

'There were televisions at the university there?' Nina asked longingly.

'Yes, three or four. Two were even colour. There was a theatre as well, where they showed old movies every Wednesday.'

'For free?'

'Yes, of course. Here, have some tea.' Radhika looked at Nina and smiled.

'But student life isn't easy there, Nina; few parents pay for college education. I worked in the mornings and studied in the evenings for the entire two and a half years. I spent all my free time at the library when I was there; I didn't have time to watch free movies or television.'

'All the same,' said Nina, 'If life is fun, I'm not afraid to work.'

'Oh, stop,' said Anila. 'Even in BA pass, you're constantly complaining. You're always making up excuses and running off from college to catch the three o'clock show. You can't stand to miss a single movie.'

Nina couldn't come up with a reply.

'That's what all my friends do.'

'All right, do have some tea,' said Radhika, as she strained the tea into everyone's cups.

11

'Some guests have come to Sahib's house,' Sonam had told her. 'He's invited you over.'

As she got ready to go to Akshay's house, Radhika wondered who these guests could be, who wanted to see her. At one point, it occurred to her that it could be Vidya, and she hesitated. But the next instant she thought that if it were Vidya, Akshay would surely have given her some warning. And anyway, Vidya was not the sort to come and stay at someone's house.

The moment she stepped into the room, she saw Rama.

'Hello Rama—Mausi,' she said politely.

Rama was leaning over, putting on her child's shoes. She looked up.

'Radhika...' She said, before falling silent. 'Oh my, you look exactly the same!'

The sitting room looked different to Radhika. There were children's toys scattered on the floor, a child seated on a chair, and a fair girl sat on Rama's lap clutching her sari.

Radhika came and sat nearby.

'This is my daughter.'

When her daughter cried out, Radhika tried to call the child over, but she hid behind her mother. Rama finished putting on her shoes and stood up. She had aged quite a bit.

'How many children do you have?' asked Radhika.

'Three! The eldest is five, he's playing outside.' Rama called to her husband, 'Did you know? Radhika's come.'

Akshay was the first to enter the room at this. He looked somewhat fatigued, but when he saw Radhika, he smiled. 'You came quickly,' he said.

'I wasn't doing anything else,' said Radhika.

'Akshay Bhaiya! Would you please call to Ayah and tell her to take the children? Then I can sit peacefully for a bit,' said Rama

The ayah came and took the children. Rama sat down near Radhika. Now she seemed to look carefully at her for the first time.

'It looks like the climate there suited you; you look radiant.'

'But that's the influence of the climate here,' objected Akshay.

'Yes, of course, she's your neighbour, after all!'

Radhika listened with a slight smile on her lips. She said nothing.

'Tell me more?' asked Rama.

'What do I have to tell? You tell me.'

Radhika felt as though the common interests they had shared as peers was now lost. They'd grown apart, which meant this situation could become a bit painful.

'What, you've been all over, doing God knows what, and you have nothing else to tell?'

Akshay was startled by how crude Rama had become; he glanced over at Radhika to see her reaction.

'Go ahead, say whatever you like! After all we're family,' said Radhika laughing. If she was offended at all, she didn't show it.

'Arre bhai, my sister has become a standard-issue snob since marrying your father. I haven't seen her for three years. When little Pappu was born, she didn't even send a letter of congratulations. But she was going through some hard things in those days. You must know.'

'No,' said Radhika.

'Your father had a severe nervous breakdown. She explained it away saying it was due to overworking but those in the know knew that it was because of you.'

Radhika blanched.

'I didn't know about the breakdown,' said Akshay.

'Oh yes, he couldn't get out of bed for months. Vidya had to take leave. You have no idea; they stayed out of the city for months. He required extensive treatment, complete rest, and nerve tonic. Truly, Radhika, you made everyone so upset.'

'And what of the shock he gave me?' retorted Radhika, her voice quavering.

Just then Rama's husband entered the sitting room and greeted Radhika loudly. He sat nearby, eyed her up and down, and asked, 'Tell me madam, how are things?'

It took Radhika some time to respond. In the meantime, Sonam brought out the tea.

Rama's husband, Kumar, was an engineer in Jamshedpur. Radhika found him a bit dull socially, but she was grateful to him for the brief respite his arrival had given her today.

'You tell me. You've been raising an army!'

'What! There are only three total. Now it's your turn to make some progress in that department. We shall accept this young bachelor, Akshay.'

Radhika could think of nothing to say after such an overt statement. She stirred her tea.

'Ask Akshay Bhaiya first, before you start making random promises,' Rama told her husband.

'Oh, I don't think it'll be that hard to convince Akshay. He's already on his own,' Kumar replied enthusiastically.

'Okay then, let's make this auspicious thing come to pass,' Rama responded with a tinge of sarcasm. Her words felt like a slap to Radhika. *Why is she behaving as an enemy towards me?* she wondered. *Maybe because of Papa...but Rama has no particular attachment to Papa.*

Kumar appeared to be enjoying the conversation. 'What say you, Akshay?' he asked.

'Please drink your tea quietly,' said Akshay. 'Sonam, bring more plates for snacks.'

Radhika glanced gratefully at Akshay. He had correctly surmised that she didn't want to continue down this path.

As they drank their tea, Rama expressed a desire to see Radhika's flat. Kumar also wanted to come along, but Rama put him off. Radhika agreed, and quietly led the way. When they arrived, Rama looked at both the rooms, then sat down on the takht. She looked quite calm at that moment.

'Papa is fine now,' said Radhika. 'I went to visit him.'

'So you saw him?'

'Yes,' replied Radhika sadly.

'But the way you went about things was so shocking. I mean it; I trembled when I heard. My husband kept asking, "Where did Radhika get so much nerve?"'

Radhika was a bit offended by her tone. 'Hundreds of people go to study abroad, what's so unique about that?' she asked.

'But very few girls run off....' Rama hesitated, perhaps in search of the right words.

'...with journalists—that's what you wanted to say, isn't it? I went of my own free will, and I wasn't dependent on anyone else.'

Rama softened a bit when she heard the vehemence of Radhika's tone. 'What do I know! You never even wrote me a line; I had to believe the rumours I heard. And in the meantime, your papa was so ill...'

The atmosphere in the room had turned unpleasant. Radhika wished Rama would just get up and leave. But she was also shocked at her behaviour. She had only fond memories of Rama during their summer in Mussoorie.

'So how do you like Akshay?' Rama asked suddenly.

'Why?'

'Sometimes he talks nonsense. Anyway it doesn't seem like Akshay's planning to get married. Ever since I got married, he's been turning down some excellent matches.'

'Really?'

Perhaps Rama could not detect the note of sarcasm in Radhika's voice.

'Yes....'

The way Rama had brought up the subject, it seemed as though she expected Radhika to ask more, but when Radhika expressed no curiosity, she changed the subject and asked, 'But tell me, why did you break up?'

'There was no relationship to begin with. Nor did I go there to start one. I went there to study, and I've come back with a degree.'

'All right then, tell me what you brought back with you,' asked Rama changing the subject. 'My husband kept telling me to write you a letter, but I didn't know your address. He had his heart set on a transistor.'

'Why? Can't you get one here?' Radhika realized her tone was abrupt, but she couldn't conceal it.

'You can get them here, but things from outside are so much better.'

'They probably are. But I brought nothing. No umbrellas, no watches, no lipsticks, no transistors. Yes, I did bring some books, some pictures, some paints. You wouldn't be interested in any of those.' Then she relented. What could poor Rama do, after all? She was only a reflection of her environment. 'If you write me a letter, I'll bring you something or other next time,' she said more sweetly.

She went into the other room and opened a suitcase of clothing she didn't need. Back in Chicago, she'd bought two nylon saris to avoid wearing her silk ones in snow and mud. She'd only worn them once or twice. She brought them out and placed them before Rama.

'If you like either of these, do take them. Or if you like them both, take them both.'

Rama flipped them over to examine them. Radhika was shocked at the look of joy on her face. *Why can I no longer enjoy such small pleasures?* she wondered.

Just then Sonam rattled the door chain.

'The children are crying for their mother,' he reported.

Radhika wrapped the saris in a newspaper and handed them to Rama. After Rama had left, she lay down on the takht. A nice breeze blew in through the window. She felt it would have been better if she hadn't seen Rama; she'd become a narrow-minded housewife. But it also made her sad that a few years of marriage could turn a cheerful, young woman so jealous and frustrated, and that she was unable to speak to a woman friend without barbs and insults.

Maybe Rama wasn't happy with married life. Below, Anila or Nina was playing a popular Western song at a high volume. At other times, Radhika would have been annoyed by a radio playing so loudly, but now, in the stillness of night, the song wafting through the air sounded just right to her.

12

Akshay and Radhika had gotten in the habit of seeing an early film on Sundays, and then lunching out. Radhika also looked forward to those days as they were a refuge from the sameness of the rest of the week. She'd found a home, but she wasn't really in the mood to work, so she spent those long, chilly days reading or thinking. How nice it felt to do nothing at all after nearly three years of hard work. Back then, she had to eat a piece of toast, drink a glass of orange juice and a cup of coffee, and run out, even if it rained or snowed. Her morning class started at seven forty-five and she was expected to get there early, before the other students.

Radhika often recollected those days. Life had been a grind of work, work, work. But what a great way to rid herself of sadness and despair. After spending every morning in class for two hours, or in the language lab, Radhika would then be free to attend her own classes, which were all in the afternoon. For two years, the routine had continued in this way, with work in the morning and study in the evening. Radhika lived in a flat with a Jewish girl named

Judith. She had taught Radhika how to save up her money, a skill that was now coming in handy. She hadn't bought a single garment for herself since it had cost quite a bit to furnish her home.

It was a Sunday filled with golden sunshine. They were seated at Vipula for lunch. The small restaurant was packed; Akshay liked Chinese food and Radhika did as well.

'Radhika!' she heard someone call out in a tone of joyful surprise.

Radhika looked up from the menu.

'Manish?' she blurted out.

'Yes, I am indeed Manish,' replied the man glancing at Akshay with curiosity.

'Akshay, this is Manish, an old acquaintance of mine,' said Radhika introducing the two. 'And this is my friend, Akshay.'

Manish smiled at the introduction, and at Akshay's invitation, sat down in one of the empty chairs.

'Manish was also at the university where I was my first year,' Radhika explained to Akshay. 'But then he went to Canada.'

'When did you get back?' Manish asked, resting his hand on the table.

'Just recently. And you?'

'It's been nearly a year for me.'

'Really? So now you're planning to live here?' Radhika asked.

'You know me, I never stick in one place for long.'

A young woman entered the restaurant and walked towards Manish with an inviting smile when she saw him.

Akshay and Manish both stood up; then there were introductions—Radhika—Karen—Akshay.

Karen took the fourth chair.

Radhika glanced over at Akshay to make sure he was amenable, but Karen had turned to speak to her. Manish smiled. Truly, nothing was hidden from Manish.

Karen wore an embroidered Kashmiri firan. She had close-cropped hair that revealed the beautiful shape of her head, a small bright forehead, light eyebrows, grey eyes, a straight nose, and beautiful, pale pink lips.

She had never seen Manish with an unattractive girl. There had been his fiancée, Vijaya, who had followed him when he'd fled India; she had been beautiful by North Indian standards; and then there had been Nayantara, the girlfriend for whom he'd broken things off with his fiancée; she looked like a yakshini carved in a column at an ancient temple; and now there was Karen.

Manish was smiling.

'How are you liking it?' Manish asked.

'Very much.'

'What are you up to, Manish?'

'An art institute opened up here last year for foreigners

coming to do research on Indian art. I'm running that, and Karen is in research training there. You?'

'Nothing right now.'

'Lady of leisure.'

'Yes, I'm liking it very much.' Radhika felt as though she were simply repeating herself.

Karen turned and started speaking to Radhika.

After lunch, they exchanged addresses before parting. When Radhika left with Akshay, she felt listless.

'You didn't get bored?' she asked him suddenly.

'No, they were interesting people.'

Stopping at the edge of the sidewalk to cross the street, Radhika said, 'Yes, I knew Manish a bit. He was an acquaintance of Dan's.'

She had dropped Dan's name into the conversation so casually. She no longer felt any pain or lingering sense of woundedness; just sadness over losing her family for the sake of Dan.

'Dan was a friend of mine.'

'Yes, Vidya told me.'

Radhika started. 'What else did Vidya tell you?'

Radhika stood still as the traffic light turned green.

'That you fell head over heels in love.'

Akshay grabbed Radhika's arm and led her across the street. Radhika walked along mechanically by his side.

It pained her deeply to know that Vidya had spoken to so many people she didn't know behind her back.

'Anything else?' she asked.

'No, but Radhika, Vidya is not as bad as she seems to you. In her heart she cares very much about you,' said Akshay.

'Probably,' Radhika responded shortly. She fell silent.

When she returned home, Radhika went and lay on the takht. Vidya must have told Akshay about her in that cold, analytical way she had; she must have told him she'd gone off with Dan and separated from him after a few months, and then lived in a state of abject poverty.

Just then her doorbell rang. She walked lazily down the stairs and opened the door, only to find Manish standing there.

'Can I come in?'

'Yes, do.'

Radhika concealed her surprise and stepped to one side to make room for him. Manish followed her, and when Radhika hesitated at the doorway, he stopped as well. She gestured towards the chairs and sat down on the takht herself.

Manish gazed approvingly at the simply decorated room and turned to look at Radhika. This was the first time he'd seen her in two or three years; she looked darker than before, and mature. More serious. A light sadness hovered about her lips.

'It's starting to get a bit warm. Can I take off my coat?'

'Yes, yes,' said Radhika.

Manish removed his coat and hung it over the back of the chair. The brilliant afternoon sunlight cast its rays across the ceiling and filled the room with a light pleasant warmth. Radhika's face looked softer in its glow.

'Shall I make coffee for you?'

'No, not yet. I just dropped Karen off in Defence Colony. I want to sit and talk to you comfortably.'

What could Radhika say? She smiled.

Manish was tall, dark and slim. There was an easy warmth to his movements. He had a long face, and a certain levity in his manner that sometimes reminded her of the innocence of a baby. Radhika felt a kind of attraction to Manish that made her somehow feel like laying her head in his lap; a schoolmate of Radhika's had actually told her the same thing about herself. Manish had no shortage of young friends, but he also bored of them quickly. Over the course of just one year, Radhika herself had seen him go through several relationships with different women.

'All right, Radhika, may I ask a personal question? Don't be offended.'

Radhika turned to look at him questioningly.

'So. Akshay?'

'Just a friend. But nowadays, he's my only friend. He's helped me a great deal. He looks after me.'

Manish laced his fingers together and laughed slightly. 'So you haven't yet changed that pattern of yours,' he said. 'You're still looking for your father among your boyfriends.'

'What do you mean?' asked Radhika, offended.

'Meaning you don't look for a lover or a husband in men. Dan took care of you during a difficult period in your life, so you began to live with him out of gratitude. Now Akshay is looking after you, so maybe you'll marry him because you want an anchor in your life, but you're not altogether willing to accept that.'

Radhika looked down. A few moments later, she replied in a muted tone, 'It's possible I'll marry Akshay. There's no room in my life for a playboy. I want a partner. Someone steady. Generous. Someone who will accept me along with all my flaws. Who will put up with my past.'

'Do you think that Akshay is that brave?'

'Only time will tell.'

A silence had spread over the room, breaking the tension.

Manish laughed. 'Forgive me, Radhika,' he said. 'We're meeting after so long, and here I am giving you a sermon. Maybe I'm getting old. But tell me, what did you do after I left for Canada?'

Then Radhika laughed too. She'd been longing to speak freely with someone; she'd figured this out on her own. She couldn't have such conversations with Akshay. Her conversations with him were limited to just a few subjects.

'Well, you were there when I separated from Dan. After that, I got a job as a Sanskrit teaching assistant. I got my MA there as well. Then I suddenly began to feel horrible living there, and I felt I couldn't find peace until I returned to India.'

'And did you find peace?' Manish smiled.

'I did not,' said Radhika sadly. 'I often think of the title of that Thomas Wolfe novel, *You Can't Go Home Again*. I've become a bit strange: I'm neither happy there nor here.'

'You said something about making coffee?' asked Manish. He got up with Radhika and stood between the two rooms. 'Somehow I get the feeling this isn't a new emotion,' he remarked. 'And I've returned after seven years.'

Radhika plugged in the percolator.

'You have family too, yes?' he asked.

'I've gone to see them all. My elder brother had gone to Calcutta with his family. I saw my stepmother at home. I saw Papa too, but...'

'He hasn't forgiven you,' finished Manish softly.

'Yes, but I didn't expect that. I thought perhaps he'd forgive me when he saw my face...'

She fell silent. Her eyes filled with tears, and she looked down. Sounds from the neighbourhood floated in the window: clothing being washed briskly down below in the courtyard, the cries of children playing ball in the park out front, the harsh voice of a woman in the rear alleyway, and hovering above all these, film tunes from the radio.

'I've brought back sad memories.' Manish rested his hand lightly on Radhika's shoulder.

'No, Manish, you don't realize how much it calms me to tell all this to a sensitive person after such a long silence; I have been suffocating, suffocating within myself...Tell me something about yourself too,' she added, handing Manish a cup of coffee. 'You have that institute.'

Manish took a sip and put down his cup. Just then, the sun was covered by a cloud and the sunlight disappeared from the room entirely.

'I told you, didn't I? It just opened last year. I got an offer for the directorship. It was quite a good one. I'd returned to India after so long, and I wanted to see how it was. After coming here, I've started to feel I'll have to decide very quickly what I'm going to do in the future. Should I marry an American girl and settle down there, or make a break from the attractions there and live in India?'

'With an American girl?'

'If she wants to live in India. But most don't like it.'

Manish picked up his cup. 'You're making coffee even better than before,' he said.

Radhika laughed. 'It's like you still remember the taste of my coffee.'

'I saw Dan in Beirut.'

'Really!' Radhika sounded unenthusiastic. She wasn't used to having someone completely leave her conscious thoughts. But Dan was now dead to her; just a forgotten memory.

'So, Radhika, if you're not doing anything these days, you should help out at our institute. Our researchers often need help from people who know Sanskrit and are bilingual, sometimes even some photography. One fellow is doing work on the vastukala of the Mughal era, Karen on the emergence and rise of Rajasthani painting, and one gentleman is photographing the shapes of the water pots from various regions in India.'

'Maybe,' said Radhika. 'Are you working on something?'

'Art history. Right now there are four or five people all together. Most of my time goes into administration. There are several assistants: two are busy making index cards, another two are taking care of the photography equipment and microfilming.'

'You're very important now.'

'Yes, Radhika,' Manish said seriously. 'I didn't want to be; but how many people are in this field abroad? I felt I had to take up the mantle of responsibility.'

'But what would I do?'

'You could sit around, all dressed up, just like you are now, in the corner of my office, and inspire us all.'

Radhika was wearing jewellery that day for the first time in a long while: a thick golden chain and a pair of earrings. Manish had probably noticed this. She blushed.

'Listen, you must have family as well?' Radhika asked.

'No, I have no one. So I have nothing to complain about. I was raised by my aunt and uncle, neither of whom are alive any longer. There is a family house in a town in Rajasthan, which will probably collapse in two or three rainy seasons.'

'The gulmohar hasn't bloomed yet, nor can the cry of the cuckoo be heard,' said Radhika for no apparent reason.

'Where did that come from?' Manish placed his empty cup down on the table and reclined comfortably in the chair with his hands behind his head. He was calm at this moment, his eyes slightly closed, his entire body relaxed. He was an easygoing person; this Radhika was realizing.

She stared at him a few times and began touching a glass bangle on her wrist.

'How can you do this?' asked Manish.

She started at his question.

'Do what?'

'This not changing. You're just the same now as you were when you disembarked from that plane at O'Hare airport: the same hairstyle, the same sweetness. I remember I went with Nayantara to greet Dan at the airport, and when I saw you walking down the stairs with him, I was filled with tremendous jealousy and anger.'

'Why anger?' Radhika burst out laughing.

'It was a natural reaction. For one thing most of the girls that go abroad are the leftovers, the unattractive ones. The ones who couldn't get married. Only a few good ones come, so why wouldn't I be angry to see a good one already taken?' There was amusement in Manish's eyes.

'I remember it well, you were wearing a pale yellow sari, extremely pale, with an orange border. Your eyes were wide with surprise; shining with delight. Dan had his arm around you, and you were taking tiny effortless steps, as though you were swimming. You didn't notice me at the airport, but that night when we arrived at Dan's flat, you were standing on the balcony. When I came out and greeted you, and you turned to look, you had this look on your face like you were lost at a fair; frightened. I almost told Nayantara that we should take you home with us. But I stopped because when you came back into the room your eyes followed only Dan.'

Radhika liked hearing all of this. This was the first time in a long while that she was hearing a man sing her praises. But she was also alert: perhaps this was simply part of Manish's bewitching charm.

'And now I see you again, and yet another gentleman appears by your side: this Akshay of yours...'

Radhika pushed a lock of hair back into her bun.

'I have great respect for Akshay.'

'But for a happy married life, respect is not enough, just as mutual physical attraction is also not enough.'

'Why do you keep bringing up marriage? I'm not in the mood to get married right now.'

'Tell me if the mood strikes you,' he replied, grabbing Radhika's hand.

'Why? Will you be the priest?'

Radhika wanted Manish to let go of her hand so she wouldn't have to withdraw it herself.

'Now look, I've ruined your entire afternoon.' Manish glanced at his watch and stood up. 'It's tea time now. Are you coming?'

'Not today, another time.' Radhika stood up as well.

'Another time, then,' he said, putting on his coat and straightening his tie.

Radhika accompanied him downstairs, and after he left, she stood staring out at the street for a long time. Her heart felt lighter, but her whole body felt fatigued from talking continuously for several hours.

13

The next time Radhika saw Manish and Karen, it was at a dinner party. It had been several months since she'd arrived in India and all her irritation had faded away. At times, she was even surprised at how quickly she'd accepted everything around her. It was true, she had done so unenthusiastically; mostly out of frustration. She'd wait in line for busses for hours and when the bus finally came, there was much pushing and shoving and selfishness. She'd ride the bus clinging to the strap, poked by elbows, her hair flying about, her toes stepped on, as she gazed through the dusty windows with dull eyes, all because Akshay had urged her to go twice a week to Deki's craft centre. She would copy down knitting patterns from foreign magazines and then teach them to Deki's knitters, and now, thanks to her, Deki had also started taking orders, and Radhika was in charge of noting down the proper measurements for various garments. Deki was grateful for Radhika's help; she wanted to open a shop for ready-made garments. But Radhika did not want to get too involved in Deki's projects, or she wouldn't have any time left for herself.

She did appreciate it when Anila sometimes also went with her, and in the meantime, Nina had somehow come to understand that there was more to life than the latest films, her favorite actor's styles and foreign-made goods; and that expatriates face hardships as well, and there is suffering all around.

Even so, Radhika was enveloped in listlessness. She continued to see Akshay, and she often received invitations from Shankar's home downstairs. Nonetheless, she felt oddly indecisive, and continued to be overwhelmed by a feeling of boredom.

Thus, she was pleasantly surprised when she received a phone call from Manish one day. Since they'd last met, she'd only received a card from Aurangabad, a single line saying all was well; then silence for several weeks. Manish casually explained that he was giving a party at his home for some friends and colleagues. That night, he sent an air-conditioned car for Radhika.

She didn't have a clear sense of the grandeur of his house until she walked inside. Outside was a large lawn surrounded by a tidy hedge and hundreds of flowerpots. The moment she entered the hallway, she saw a long veranda, and beyond that, wide-open steps of white stone, followed by a courtyard, and then a lawn edged with a thicket of banana palms. Cane furniture was set out on the veranda, where many people sat or reclined.

The veranda was flooded with moonlight and candles flickered in candlesticks. Manish stood up when he saw her. He came over and warmly clasped her hands.

'Radhika! Good to see you,' he said. Then he introduced her to the others: 'Jean, Nisha, Lawrence, Marcus, Rodney, Lara, Pravin, Divakar, Helen, Kumar, and Kris!'

Radhika greeted them all and sat down on an empty stool.

'What will you have?' Manish asked, leaning towards her.

'What is everyone else having?'

'Manhattans, martinis, bourbon, scotch on the rocks; I'm drinking a Bloody Mary.'

'Then I'll have the same,' said Radhika.

In a short while, a uniformed bearer respectfully handed her a glass. It looked like a glass of cold tomato juice, but when Radhika took a sip, she realized there was quite a bit of vodka in it. Glass in hand, she listened to the conversation. It seemed that Lawrence was an archeologist; he had returned after several months on a dig in Rajasthan. Jean was describing his trip to South India extensively to Divakar. Radhika looked over at Kris, that is, Krishna. She wore a long, silk, Western cloak-shaped garment with metallic embroidery on the high neck, but you can't hide the hues of an Indian face. She spoke in an authentic Boston accent to a young man seated by her, '...So Pravin's boss asked me...with soda...no...I said, just rye with a little bit of ice...so Pravin's boss said, Pravin, your wife can really hold her liquor. I had no idea; now I'll have to raise your salary!' She cast a contemptuous glance at Nisha's glass. Nisha was obviously drinking Coca Cola.

Karen came outside after a little while. She was wearing a batik print dress of a shade that melted into the darkness. She looked at Radhika, smiled and came over to her.

'Indian servants are so slow. Dinner still isn't ready, despite my best efforts. Do you have the same problem?'

'Not that I know of. That problem has never come up for me.'

'They must think I'm inexperienced and do it to annoy me,' sighed Karen.

It was clear from Karen's manner that she was the lady of the house. As she spoke with Radhika, Karen kept glancing at Manish, who was speaking with Jean.

Radhika sat amidst the hushed conversations in a white chikan sari, embroidered with tiny pink vines. She felt self-contained, holding the smooth coolness of the glass in her hand, not allowing the slightest hint of her inner torment to show on her face. She watched Karen and Jean and Lawrence. She'd lived in their country, but once she realized she could never be a part of it, she had been eager to cut ties and flee. And now here she was in her own country, but where were her people? Were Manish, Pravin, Kris, and she herself representing this country in any way at all? It seemed to Radhika that they were all puppets and had grown accustomed to behaving a particular way. Wearing a mask of sophistication, bored with life, dissatisfied, restless. Where did all these emotions take them? Into Karen's arms, into a glass of rye, and...and...into that feeling of protection she had in Akshay's presence.

Radhika felt relieved that Manish had not told her to bring Akshay along. Akshay was a high-level worker in a foreign firm, but he was, at heart, as Indian as a bowl of kheer, or Holi red, or paan. Akshay was nice, even if one did not feel a thrill in his embrace, but he would give his wife every comfort, he'd be a good father to his children. Not like Manish, who...Radhika again recalled Vijaya's sad, dull face. Vijaya, who had chased after Manish from India, and of whom Manish had said coldly, 'I no longer feel the same way about her.' And now Karen. How long would she be able to hold onto Manish?

Manish walked over and placed a hand on Karen's shoulder. 'You're quiet, Radhika,' he said.

When Manish was near, she was aware of his presence the way she was aware of her own heart beating when she was excited. Manish wasn't merely physically attractive. Even when he smiled unseriously, a small machine was probably ticking away in his mind, assessing all the people around him. He hadn't become an associate professor at an American university or the director of this art institute for no reason. What must he be like in serious moments? Radhika was suddenly curious. Until now, she'd only known him in a particular guise, as a social butterfly. But what of the Manish behind all that?

Radhika felt annoyed at herself. An unimaginative mind dwells upon the affairs of other people.

A little while later, Divakar came and sat by her. 'Now I'll talk to this one,' he said to Manish.

'Be my guest.' Manish smiled. 'But be careful with Divakar, Radhika, he's the leader of the Dissatisfied Indians Association.'

'This Manish has become hard-hearted,' said Divakar. 'He hasn't the slightest sympathy for his fellow countrymen. You see his attitude. If it were me, I'd shrink with shame.' He spoke in jest, and Radhika took his words as such.

'If Divakar starts weeping over his woes, call the bearer and have him refill his glass,' suggested Manish as he left.

Divakar stared at her for a moment. 'Are you connected with Manish's work?' he asked.

'No, I'm not,' replied Radhika succinctly. 'And you?'

'I'm a lecturer at a degree college. I have a doctorate in physics from McGill University.'

Radhika didn't ask anything further. It was obvious Divakar had returned to India after three or four years of hard work, and his college, instead of giving him a high rank, hadn't even been able to give him annual advancement.

'My wife says we should sacrifice for our country. We should live in our own country; we should consider the future of our children. My Canadian professor has already written several letters to me, but my wife says I should stay here. She's a simple, lovely woman. But I ask, is my country the right place for the work I plan to do? My children aren't getting into good schools. I have to wait years to buy a decent scooter, my salary isn't high enough to invite a few friends over and serve them good liquor, or to keep a servant so that at least I won't have to stand in line and wait for milk. By contrast, look at Manish, or over there—Pravin and Kris—and my wife says...'

Just then, Karen approached them. 'Come, Radhika,'

she said. 'I'll show you the house. You come too, Divakar...'

Radhika stood up awkwardly. Divakar smiled. He waved his hand. 'Do go and take a look at Manish's home,' he said, closing his eyes.

Manish had turned three of the larger rooms into an office. There were also three guest rooms for people coming through town. But even after all that, there was quite a bit of room left. Radhika felt obligated to be polite to Karen, despite feeling uninterested. By the time the two of them returned, the guests had begun walking into the dining room.

Radhika was seated at the dining table with a young, American man to her right, and Pravin to her left. She usually found the sort of formal conversation one has with a new acquaintance quite dull, but on such occasions, one just had to be polite.

The young man held out the salad bowl so Radhika could serve herself.

'I'm Rodney,' he said. 'Rodney Moore. I've come here on a Fulbright.'

Radhika took two small pieces of red tomato, a long piece of shaved mooli, and a green pepper. 'My name is Radhika,' she said. 'I stayed in your country for a few years. I've been back here for some months now.'

When Radhika reached out to take the salad bowl, their fingers touched for an instant, but there was no thrill to the touch, as though their fingers were made of plasticine. Radhika handed the bowl to Pravin on her other side.

'How did you like our country?' asked Rodney.

The same cliché question. Etiquette demanded one respond with a sigh, 'I loved it!' But Radhika felt awkward on such occasions, so she replied simply, 'It's a lovely place.'

As she spoke, images of America ran rapidly through her mind like a film reel: the California coastline; the mountains of Colorado; rivers, brilliant green fields, flowering trees, fall foliage, and falling snow.

Rodney smiled.

'And how do you like our country?' asked Radhika.

Rodney paused a moment before speaking.

'Very interesting. Very.'

Americans always say such things to avoid unpleasant topics. Radhika knew this. Nonetheless, she stuck with the topic as she lightly sprinkled her salad with salt.

'Interesting in what sense?'

'Well, take Bombay for example,' Rodney said, speaking slowly. 'When you see all those slums on the way from the airport into the city, it confirms so many of your preconceptions about India. Don't be offended, but the portrayal of India we see...'

'...and which is all thanks to Western journalists,' Radhika interrupted bitterly.

Rodney now held out the plate of cutlets for her. Radhika took one, then held the plate herself so Rodney could serve himself.

'After the trip from the airport,' Rodney continued, 'when we arrived in the city, it didn't seem like a poor country at all. Large cars, women wearing sparkling diamond earrings, restaurants full of people, endless shopping.'

Radhika cut off a bite of cutlet with her fork, dipped it in the tomato sauce, and popped it in her mouth.

'And Indian values—don't be offended—it's hard to walk down the street without someone following you, and if you didn't know the words "*change money change money*" in any Indian language, you'd think *change money* was an Indian greeting.'

Radhika laughed slightly.

'And it's the same in Delhi. An Indian friend told me that girls from good families...'

'I don't believe it,' said Radhika firmly. 'Anyway, you know such evils can be found anywhere if you go looking for them. You must have seen the poor sections of Chicago, and you must know the state of morals in high schools and colleges there too.'

'But there's a big difference in those? In our culture, friendship between a woman and a man is considered very natural, very genuine. It's a method for finding a life partner. But if you do that for money, it comes into another category and then we don't make a huge display of our spiritual knowledge. Okay, we are materialists, and we accept that.'

Radhika had finished her cutlet. She couldn't come up with an immediate response to this. 'Well,' she said, 'this all stems from Western materialism.' But then she changed the topic, so the conversation wouldn't turn bitter and unpleasant. 'And where have you travelled?' she asked.

Perhaps Rodney had also had enough, because he didn't reply to Radhika's question and began speaking to the young woman on his left. Pravin was sitting on Radhika's other side. After a long silence, he asked, 'Did you get your degree in journalism?'

'No, in fine arts,' said Radhika.

'Really!' replied Pravin with surprise. 'I heard your former husband was a famous journalist, that's why I thought...'

'How interesting!' Radhika said in an American accent. 'What part of India are you from?'

'The northern part.'

Then Radhika started replying to his Boston English in Hindi. After a few sentences, the situation grew comical. Pravin must have noticed this as well, for he said, 'I've got out of the habit of speaking Hindi.'

'It's only natural.'

'Our children don't know any other language besides English.'

'You must be proud of that.'

Pravin stared at her briefly and then turned to the woman seated on his other side.

Saved from her dining companions, Radhika turned her attention towards dessert: ice cream with strawberries. *So you can get strawberries here now*, she thought suddenly. The snow must have melted by now back there, and people must be swimming in the cold waters of the lake.

The guests were now standing up for coffee. Radhika also came and stood on the veranda. The banana trees were still bathed in moonlight. Suddenly, Radhika's heart felt terribly heavy. When Manish came and stood by her, she blurted out, 'Such boring people I sat between, I've got a headache.'

'Poor girl,' Manish said affectionately. 'Come, let's stroll about the garden a while, your headache will go away.'

Radhika glanced over at the guests who were emerging from the dining room one at a time.

'Karen will look after them,' said Manish.

The guests crossed the hallway and emerged in the moonlight, where there was also a slight chill in the air.

Radhika sighed deeply.

'The mehndi is blooming.'

'Yes, it's close by,' said Manish.

For a little while, they strolled along the path paved with square, white stones, then Radhika took off her sandals.

'I'm going to sit on the grass,' she said.

'Come over here, then. The front section was watered just this evening, Radhika,' said Manish.

They had walked over to the side lawn, which was bounded by the property wall. The far side of the house was covered in thick vines, and behind stood another thicket of banana trees. There was also a swing.

'A swing!'

Radhika clapped her hands like a child, running towards it excitedly.

'Will you swing?' asked Manish.

Radhika felt embarrassed by Manish's curiosity.

'No.' She sat down. 'You're living very grandly, Manish,'

she added after a moment. 'Such a large house...so many servants.'

The lines on Manish's face were softened in the moonlight.

'It's okay,' he said softly.

'That Pravin is a strange one. He was calling Dan my former husband.'

Manish was silent.

'When are you thinking of returning?' she asked.

'I keep wondering whether I should go back or not. The longer I remain abroad, the more difficult it will be to return to India and settle down.'

'So are you thinking of settling down in India?' she asked with surprise.

'I said, didn't I, that I haven't been able to decide.' Manish leaned back on his elbows and stared off into the distance. 'All the running around is wearing me out. I have success, but even with wealth, I've found no peace.'

'Will Karen want to stay in India?'

'I haven't asked her yet. Karen's a nice girl, but...'

'Manish, will you always be like this?' asked Radhika accusingly.

'No, Radhika,' said Manish softly, 'I'm more serious than I was before. But yes, I'm ashamed of how I treated Vijaya. I could have done that without wounding her.'

Radhika was silent for a while as she picked at blades of grass and nibbled on them.

'I got your card from Aurangabad.'

'You did? I sent it so you wouldn't think that I'd just disappeared.'

'The thought had occurred to me.' Then, after a silence, she added 'Let's go inside now. Karen must be looking for you.'

She started to get up, but Manish grabbed her hand and pulled her back down.

'There are very few people inside that would be aware that they should be worrying about us.'

'But what about Karen?'

'I have a right to sit and chat with whomever I wish in my own home, Radhika.'

'Hmmm...'

'Why are you getting nervous?'

'I'm not,' said Radhika.

Manish stubbed out his cigarette and moved closer to Radhika. He put his arms around her slowly, perhaps waiting to see her reaction, but she pushed him away and stood up.

'Manish, I don't want to get involved again,' she said. In that single instant, Radhika realized she'd been expecting a situation like this, consciously or not, ever since she'd re-encountered Manish.

Sounds of laughter came from the house. The fragrance of mehndi floated through the air. Radhika felt warmed by Manish's touch, after so long without any contact with a man. But she did not turn to look at him.

14

Early the next morning, Radhika's doorbell rang. When she opened the door, she saw the Mallika flower delivery van. The driver handed her a huge bouquet and drove off. Radhika had to go to Prema, cradling the long stem gladiolas in her arms, to ask for a tall vase.

Anila and Nina crowded around her.

'How lovely! How sweet!' they cried.

'Who sent them? Where did they come from?' asked Nina.

'They're from a friend,' Radhika replied. Though they'd come without a card, she knew no one besides Manish could have sent her flowers.

As she arranged the flowers in her room, memories of the past night returned to her afresh. She'd been surprised at her own firmness and a bit pleased too. In the bright sunlight of morning, she felt she'd made the right decision. Before this, she'd always simply gone with the flow of her feelings; she'd never thought about where the current might carry her. All the same, Akshay's star had faded a bit before

Manish. Certainly, he lacked Manish's sophistication, but he wasn't fickle either.

After she'd arranged the flowers, Radhika gazed at them from different angles for a while. Suddenly, she felt sad. She lay back down on the takht and covered her face.

She lay like this all morning. It was a Sunday, but for several weeks, her routine of going out with Akshay seemed to have broken down; for one thing, there had been no good new movies for a while, and for another, Akshay had grown extremely busy at the office. Occasionally, Radhika went over to see him and found Sonam there alone. The previous Sunday, Deki had come to see Radhika. She'd brought momos and the two of them had sat together eating Tibetan food.

Around eleven o'clock, she heard Nina calling out to her. She had a phone call. It was Manish, who wanted to know if she was free. Radhika thought for a moment, then decided she'd spend her Sunday with him.

She got ready, lost in thought, left a note for Akshay that she wasn't free today, and went out. Manish was waiting for her at Vipula.

He smiled. 'Come, have a seat.'

'I hoped you'd be free today,' he said when she had sat down. 'All the same, I thought I'd call first and ask.'

'Akshay is very busy these days,' said Radhika. She refused coffee in favour of Coca Cola.

'Are you somewhere far away right now, Radhika?'

'Me? No. I'm right here. Just thinking,' said Radhika. 'Your party was very successful yesterday,' she said politely.

'Everyone stayed until three o'clock; only you left early,' he said, but there was no reproach in his tone.

'I'm out of the habit...'

'...of staying up late at parties, or coping with fans?' Now he sounded irritated.

'Both,' said Radhika. 'And you are perhaps always rehearsing,' she added.

'I was completely serious.'

'Why? Have you had enough of Karen?' Radhika asked sarcastically. But then, she felt ashamed. She sipped her Coca Cola through a straw.

'Karen is my student,' said Manish. 'What on earth are you on about today?'

'I'm sorry,' said Radhika. She felt abashed. Manish had invited her out. And here she was saying bitter, petty things. A little later they left Vipula and strolled a while in the dusty haze down a street lined with cotton trees. Radhika wore a cotton Bengali sari and a sleeveless blouse. Her hair was loose. As always, she wore no jewellery or makeup besides a colourless lipstick, which left only a faint glow on her lips.

Manish adapted himself to Radhika's mood, saying pleasant things to her in a quiet, polite voice. Radhika noticed that his eyes were bright and full of reverent attraction.

Radhika's feet were covered in dust and even her yellow sari border had turned grey. She stopped by the side of the street, and Manish hailed a passing taxi.

'Friend's Colony,' he said to the taxi driver.

Radhika started but didn't say anything.

Fine, she thought. *Manish's house is fine*. How long can we keep strolling about on the road?

'What happened to your car?' Radhika asked as the taxi set off.

'It's gone to Palam to drop off Lawrence,' said Manish.

The house looked even grander in the dazzling sunlight. Several servants emerged when they heard them come in: the gardener, the chaprasi, and the bearer.

Manish brought Radhika into the living room. She sighed with relief in the chill of the air-conditioning and walked over to the sofa.

'I've never seen such a large brass table,' said Radhika, touching the round table in the middle of the room.

She sat down, and when Manish sat by her, she remarked, 'Everything in this house is king-sized. You're living like a king in all this grandeur,' said Radhika. She stood up again, suddenly agitated.

'Am I hearing a bit of envy in your tone?'

'Not a little. Lots. Lots and lots.'

'Why, Radhika, why are you so down?' asked Manish. Something about his tone made Radhika return to the sofa. She felt as though she couldn't tolerate any more just now.

Manish left the room for a little while, perhaps to give some orders to the bearer.

When he returned, he sat by Radhika, quite close. Radhika lay back where she was. Manish put his arm around her and turned her face towards him.

'What is it, Radhika, that you haven't told me? What's bothering you?'

'Everything,' said Radhika. She fell silent for a while, fearing she was so overwhelmed with emotions, she might burst into tears.

'Everything,' she said, more able to control herself. 'My family, the environment, the meaninglessness of my life, and me, myself...what I'm becoming, just an emotionless puppet...'

'Who told you you're were becoming emotionless? Your problem is that your emotions are your driving...'

Radhika removed herself from Manish's arm and stood up once more. He made no attempt to get up, and lit a cigarette.

'Maybe you're still suffering from reverse culture shock, Radhika.'

'Who knows!' she said quietly.

Manish stood up as well and went over to her. Radhika stared fixedly at the rows of petunias outside the French doors that opened onto the lawn.

'When we leave our country and go abroad, we spend the first six months in culture shock. This makes us constantly put our own country, our own culture, on a pedestal. But then we get used to living in that country. After two or more years of living there, we become accustomed to its ways, so when we return to our own country, we get a second shock: reverse culture shock.'

'Did that happen to you as well?' asked Radhika.

'Yes, Radhika. I wasn't prepared for it. I returned after seven years, but some things still bothered me. I kept wanting to scream at someone and ask, "Why haven't you people made any healthy progress?" Granted, we are backwards, but we could at least be cultured and polite. We could banish our ignorance and laziness. But no, what happens here is that anyone who makes something of themselves is punished for it in equal measure. I had to go to great trouble to free my photography equipment from customs. I was running around in circles. At the beginning, so many things bothered me: the rudeness of taxi drivers, the irresponsibility of my own staff. But these are all small things we eventually adapt to. Things have improved now.'

'How so?'

'I paid the custom duty and got my photography equipment back. Once I got a car, I started taking taxis much less, and hardened my heart regarding the irresponsible people on my staff.'

There was a tap on the door and the bearer entered carrying two delicate long-stemmed glasses on a tray. Tiny drops of water condensed on the sides of the glasses, which could not have contained more than a sip.

'Here you go, Radhika, it's Aquavit, that is, aab-e-hayaat, the elixir of immortality.'

'Aab-e-hayaat?'

'Yes, when I was coming home via Denmark, I bought a bottle.'

Manish emptied his glass in one gulp and returned it to the tray. Radhika watched and did the same.

'Uff, I'm wasted,' she exclaimed. 'It's really something, this aab-e-hayaat of yours.'

Manish laughed as he waved the bearer away.

'What, don't you like it?' he asked.

Drops of perspiration glistened on Radhika's forehead. 'No, I do,' she said, wiping them away.

'At the very least, you must be feeling less tense. If I gave you a pill, you wouldn't take it, and then you'd sit around all day with your muscles tensed up, like the over-tightened strings on an instrument.'

And truly, the afternoon did seem to pass swiftly. After lunch, she went into Manish's office and examined the art objects collected for the institute: a Shridevi statue from the eleventh century, the wheels of a broken chariot from a southern temple, some lovely miniature paintings, and various photos of Indian pots taken by Rodney. After that, they returned to the living room, and Manish put on a record of a Beethoven symphony. Radhika reclined on the sofa, resting her arm along the back, her head bowed, lazy, drowsy, and rather happy.

15

The next morning, birds, perhaps doves, flew about in the sky, their wings shimmering like silver in the sunlight, the fragrance of fresh coffee filled the room, but Radhika's heart was heavy. Her thoughts kept returning to Akshay, though she tried to push them away. When she'd returned from Manish's, a note from Akshay had awaited her: *'I was about to come over when I got your message. Here are some matinee tickets. As soon as you get back, let me know, I'll be at home.'* But it was already growing dark by the time Radhika had returned, and when she'd gone over to Akshay's house, he'd been tired and irritable, and that had made her feel a bit ashamed of herself.

After strolling about the roof for a while, Radhika bathed, changed her clothes, and fixed her hair so she could swing by the bazaar.

'You haven't visited us for so long,' Prema complained when she went downstairs. Prema was buying vegetables. Radhika said nothing; she just smiled. The woman selling the vegetables had unconsciously arranged the green peas and carrots in her basket in a decorative manner so they'd look aesthetically pleasing.

Radhika walked a short distance, but then her heart sank. There were enormous crowds of office workers crammed at every bus stop.

She felt completely cut off from this crowd, from all the commotion and bustle; she was no longer a part of her own environment. She felt like an outsider even when she lived here. Her life was an aimless journey, a long dark tunnel. Two years before, this knowledge had motivated her quite a bit, but that had been a different environment, a different culture; living there, the feeling of separation seemed normal and natural. She'd thought perhaps that when she returned to her homeland, amidst her own people, the icicle inside her would melt. But now that seemed impossible. She was performing the daily tasks of life mechanically, and her restlessness and ennui continued to grow.

Radhika walked along the street. The houses here were bounded by low walls. She read the nameplates on the gates. There was a grand mansion belonging to a lawyer, decorated with pots of blue, mark-two chrysanthemums, and green asparagus; after that, a lady doctor's lovely, modern one-storey house, which had been ruined by a cement lattice. The lattice was painted red ochre. The doctor must have been quite wealthy as she had a long, American car parked in her garage. Radhika walked a bit further to where the street veered left. Here there was an endless stream of busses, cars, and scooters, all in a mad rush to reach their destination.

Radhika walked straight ahead. A tent was pitched in an empty field. It belonged to a small school, where a young woman teacher irritably watched a group of children playing. The children ran around in circles in a cloud of dust, many pairs of skinny legs chasing after one another, the girls' oiled braids flying behind them. Ahead lay deserted hills dotted with thorny shrubs; the ruins of two tombs stood nearby. Radhika climbed the steps of a tomb. The ground was neat and clean up there. She sat on a stone step. From that slight slope, she could see the entire city spread out before her. The stillness rolled towards her across the hills. She sat for a long time.

16

The two of them seemed to have nothing to say to one another. Their lunch passed in silence. Vinay looked up at Radhika periodically. Radhika was serious, lips pursed, motionless and withdrawn.

She'd been surprised, even a little pleased, to receive a phone call from her brother. His family feeling had not died completely. Now he was seated across the table from her, eating. He hadn't changed much in the past few years, although he seemed a bit more relaxed with Bhabhi not there. They'd dispensed with the various formalities and now there was nothing left to say. His business was going well. The children were fine. Papa was writing his book in the house across the Ganga. He had Bhavani there to look after him. Radhika was living in a small flat in a crowded colony doing nothing. All she did with her free time was stare at her sunflower print and think.

They were both almost done eating. Vinay would return to Lucknow on a morning flight. Now that their conversation had ended, Radhika just stared at the Mughal-style decorations on the hotel dining room walls.

'Try to come soon. Your bhabhi wants to see you.'

'Okay,' said Radhika without argument, although she knew that for the time being, she had no intention of leaving Delhi. Perhaps Vinay knew this as well.

'Vinay, I'm going home now,' Radhika said when dinner was over.

Vinay stared at her for a moment, then called for a car. The shrubberies on the hotel lawn were draped with twinkling blue lights, creating a festive ambiance.

There was a chill in the air.

The car that Vinay had rented for his stay came and stopped by the bushes. A long Mercedes. Radhika said goodbye and got in the car.

Vinay turned to leave, then returned, and held out a thick envelope.

'I don't need it right now,' said Radhika, stopping him. 'If I do, I'll ask.'

The car set out. She reclined in the backseat and began to think about Vinay. Did all that wealth not make him feel lonely? But he'd made success his life's goal. And Papa was living in that empty mansion, and she in her noisy flat...

The car stopped in front of the house. The Shankar family was seated on chairs on the lawn. Akshay was there as well.

Shankar called out to Radhika respectfully.

'Akshay, I haven't seen you in a while,' said Radhika.

'Yes, there's been a lot more work lately. It's the end of the year, you see.'

'My brother came.'

'Yes, I know,' said Akshay.

There was something in Akshay's manner that Radhika couldn't quite put her finger on. He seemed withdrawn.

Inside, the telephone rang.

Radhika felt as though Akshay's eyes were glued to her back as she rose to go inside after Anila had called out to her. It was Manish. He'd returned just that afternoon and had been trying to get Radhika on the phone the whole evening. Now he wanted to know if she could come out for a cup of coffee.

Radhika had been trying to keep from drowning in a flood of sorrow ever since she'd parted from Vinay and returned home, and now Akshay's withdrawn behaviour had pushed her under. Radhika hesitated for a moment as she held the phone in her hand.

'So, I'll come and get you?' asked Manish.

'Okay!' she agreed.

She returned to the lawn and picked up her purse from the chair.

'Sit a while longer,' urged Prema.

'Some other time,' said Radhika.

She went upstairs. The room felt close, so she opened the windows. All was quiet in the huts of the neighbours who'd been kicking up a ruckus all day long. Far off, she could hear a flute playing *sa re ga ma*, but by the time the sound reached her it turned tuneless. The player however, was determined—every time he started anew, and when he arrived on *ma* yet again, the same distorted note rang out.

Radhika stood by the window now, thinking about

nothing in particular. The sky outside was a deep grey. The brilliant Milky Way now lay in the heavens. The Pahari servant was washing the dishes below in the courtyard.

Just then Manish arrived at her open door.

'Arre, you got here so quickly!'

'Yes, I called you from the nearby drugstore. Are you ready?'

Radhika didn't want to look at his face. She moved away from the window.

'Yes. But sit for a moment. Have some coffee here.'

Manish sat down. He opened his cigarette case and took out a cigarette.

'I didn't expect you'd return so early; by ten o'clock, that is.'

'Vinay, my elder brother, is visiting. He's leaving tomorrow morning.'

'Ah, you have a family, Radhika?'

Radhika remained serious, though she realized Manish was teasing her.

'Yes, I have an elder brother, father, mausi, nephews, nieces, everyone...'

'You're lucky. I have no one.'

'Really?'

'Of course.'

Manish's face was grave, but Radhika wasn't sure if he was truly serious, or if the gravity was merely masking laughter.

'Okay, let's go,' said Radhika.

When the two of them went downstairs, everyone, including Akshay, was still sitting out on Shankar's lawn.

17

Sonam brought in dinner, and Akshay dined. But he was not at ease. He kept thinking about Manish and Radhika. The unbearable distress that chafed at his heart was unfamiliar to him. Many years ago, he had liked Rama, but he'd shied away from marriage. He could not understand the change occurring within him now. Young women he'd known for ages had suddenly started appearing beautiful to him. Deki's lovely skin, Anila's eyes, he even found himself frequently attracted to the carefree Nina. But Radhika was the most desirable of all.

He was fond of Radhika and felt he could spend his life with her. On several occasions, he'd had an irrepressible desire to take her in his arms when she was close by, but each time some unconscious hesitation stopped him. Sometimes, when Radhika was laughing, or he could tell that she was enjoying his company, all the things Vidya had said began to eat away at him.

The truth was that he could not forget that Radhika had lived openly, like a wife, with that journalist for a year, and that after that, who knows how many more there had been over the next two years...he couldn't ask Radhika about this directly, but whenever she met up with a former acquaintance, he felt a sting of doubt. When he saw their friendly behaviour, he couldn't help but wonder whether Manish had also been a lover of Radhika's.

It wasn't that he felt unashamed of his own pettiness. Sometimes, Radhika seemed so pure, so untouched, so full of virginal bashfulness. Akshay saw her face, as serene as the moonlight, and felt confused. He felt that everything he'd heard about her was false. The truth was this: Radhika's grave tranquility, her shiny unadorned forehead and pulled back hair, her light bow-shaped eyebrows and her large eyes illuminated by an unusual beauty, her small straight nose, and her oval face.

Nonetheless, Akshay couldn't muster the courage to fully accept Radhika along with her past. He often felt ashamed of this, but now that he was older, he desired the sort of wife who would be his alone: young and just a bit educated—someone like Nina or Deki.

Akshay smiled to himself. What, that mad carefree Nina, whose orhni always slid down her arms, really?

Akshay's windows were briefly illuminated by the headlights of a car. He had drawn near the window in the darkness.

So Radhika had returned.

18

The dark purple petunias had begun to wither in the flowerbeds and the jacaranda tree near the crowded street had blossomed. Radhika had no need to count how many months had gone by since she'd returned. Each day that passed had left its mark on her memory. When she'd arrived, it had been pleasant to sit outside and sun herself, but now the sunlight was intolerable. In just a short while, her upstairs rooms would start to bake; but how would it feel when the first sprinkling of rain fell? She would hear the drops of falling rain on the lower roofs. Radhika liked rain. But there were still many days until the monsoon; first these dusty, baking days must pass.

Manish had gone travelling somewhere again; Bombay, perhaps. Sometimes Radhika felt his absence, especially in the evenings, after spending an entire day alone. It was then that she felt like sitting on the open roof and having pleasant conversations. Anila and Nina rarely came upstairs. Prema never at all. She could watch the comings and goings of people nearby as she strolled about the roof: the children playing below, a neighbour woman walking by with a new pot in her hand, and over there, in the hutments, the increasing bustle.

That day, Radhika was returning from the bookshop. Whenever she felt depressed, she liked to read novels—usually something light. She carried a brown packet of murder mysteries: two novels by John Dixon Carr she'd picked out from a pile of old books being sold on the pavement. As she climbed the stairs, she heard Akshay's voice coming from Shankar's room. She didn't stop but went upstairs to put coffee on the stove. She began to straighten up the room, taking down the saris hanging on the line and folding them up. Then she fixed her hair and sat down on a low chair.

In a little while, the sharp fragrance of coffee began to waft through the room and when she looked out the open door, she found that it was slightly dark outside.

When she went downstairs, Shankar's living room was empty. The Pahari told her that they'd all gone out on a stroll as far as Akshay's house. Radhika hesitated, then set out in the same direction. Everyone was at the gate. They fell silent when they saw her. Had they been talking about her?

Radhika felt she'd been wrong to come, but if Akshay was surprised to see her, he didn't show it.

'Radhika,' he said, 'I haven't seen you in ages. Come, come upstairs.'

'All right, we'll say goodbye now,' said Shankar.

'I've come out to take a walk,' said Radhika. 'I'll come another time.'

Radhika first learned of Akshay's imminent departure from Sonam. She was stunned when he told her Akshay would be moving to Dalhousie. He'd been transferred to Calcutta. It was true that for the past several weeks, she hadn't seen any sign of him at all; but she'd simply accepted the story that he was swamped at work.

'When is he going?' she asked.

'This Saturday,' Sonam replied, drying his hands.

That is, the day after tomorrow, thought Radhika. *So soon*.

'Is Sahib at home now?' she asked.

'He's visiting downstairs,' said Sonam. Radhika went to change her sari before going downstairs, but then she stopped. If Akshay wanted, he could come up. It occurred to her that he'd started visiting downstairs quite often, but he had no time to come up to see her. Radhika didn't want to be offended, so she picked up a book and lay down on her bed to read. Although a corpse had already appeared just a few pages before in the inner chambers of the Chinese pot-making factory, Radhika didn't feel like reading any further.

So, Akshay was leaving.

When he didn't come upstairs that day either, Radhika felt he must be angry with her for some reason. But she couldn't imagine any reason for his anger. She kept thinking about her interactions with Akshay, but couldn't recall any occasion that would have offended him. If anyone should be angry, it was Radhika, since Akshay had been ignoring her for who knows how long. He visited downstairs and then went away. Radhika wanted to forget about it and go for a walk, but she couldn't bring herself to do it. That unanswered question kept digging at her like a thorn. And so Friday had passed by. Radhika had gone to the bazaar that day, just to distract herself a bit. But there too she wandered about restlessly. Then Saturday came.

19

Should she go to see Akshay, she wondered. She couldn't make up her mind. She really was surprised by his behaviour. That day, Nina had come upstairs and told her that Akshay was leaving by plane on Sunday morning. Nina stayed to chat for a while, but the whole time Radhika kept secretly wishing she'd leave.

As Nina sat there, Radhika suddenly decided that if Akshay really was leaving, let him; she wouldn't go to bid him farewell herself. True, in the beginning, she'd been grateful to him, but now it was clear he was behaving like a sulky child. Nina had come to invite her to dinner. Radhika agreed to come although she didn't want to. She knew that he would be there as well.

Akshay had already arrived when she came downstairs. He sat holding a glass of tomato juice, looking a bit sad. Radhika had decided that if Akshay was going to live far away and behave coldly, she would do the same. But she was completely taken aback by the way he smiled when he saw her. She stared right into his eyes and then looked away, unable to stand it.

Did Akshay...? Does Akshay...? Radhika wondered. His gaze was neither sulky nor childish. Had she hurt Akshay in some way? And then suddenly she was struck with a realization.

Manish!

Radhika felt such a sense of relief, she wanted to stand up and laugh. When Anila had given her a glass of pineapple juice, she went and stood by him. As though the two of them were meeting for the first time in years.

'So, you're leaving tomorrow?' Radhika asked. She took a sip of juice; its bitter sweetness was pleasant.

'I am!' said Akshay. He stared at her.

'Your transfer was so sudden.'

'Yes! They had room for me there in the head office.'

Nina came and sat on the arm of Akshay's chair. 'Definitely invite us to visit after you get there!' she said.

'Of course,' he replied. Once more he gazed at Radhika. When Nina had come over, Radhika had moved away and now stood with her eyes fixed on the mantelpiece. Her face was serious, her lips motionless, and once more Akshay felt as he gazed at her in profile that the shape of her face was completely flawless.

Had he been unjust to her? Should he have spoken clearly to her? Akshay imagined himself saying to Radhika, 'Look, Radhika, I'm very attached to you, I want you to be my wife, but subconsciously, I couldn't accept you completely from the beginning. I can't stop thinking about your past. Tell me, Radhika, was Manish also your lover...?'

Akshay knew full well how Radhika would react to that. No, he would keep quiet. If he said all this, Radhika wouldn't allow him to be angry and hurt. This was his own small-mindedness, and he would endure it himself.

All the same, why did he feel so confused? The more he steered clear of Radhika, the more he felt she overshadowed his life. He doubted he could successfully keep his distance and get rid of her.

Akshay ate dinner mechanically. Prema kept saying how sad she was that he was leaving, Anila's face was heavily made up and expressionless as always, Nina's conversation was a meaningless thicket, and Radhika was totally silent.

Radhika's silence made Akshay anxious. He was also distressed by the fear his departure might be of no importance to her, and this made him eager to get her alone for a few moments.

After dinner, everyone sat outside for a while. The atmosphere had become rather tense, and Akshay kept getting the feeling he'd made Radhika angry, and that not just she, but everyone, felt this way.

It was Radhika who first excused herself.

'What will you do if you go upstairs? Do sit a bit longer!' Prema pressed.

Radhika ran her finger along the cane back of the chair. 'No,' she said. 'I'm starting to get a headache. I think I'll go now.'

She said goodbye to Akshay, thanked Prema for the delicious meal, and went upstairs, where she paced around the roof dejectedly. The breeze had died, and now it was extremely humid. A cloud of dust nearly covered the faint light of the stars.

Radhika looked down as she stood, resting her elbow on the parapet, not with any particular aim, nor out of curiosity. The chair Akshay had been sitting in was now empty. So after she'd left, he hadn't stayed either. But why had he become like this? The question gnawed at Radhika. After walking around on the roof, she turned on the light in her room and picked up the book lying on the bed. She was uninterested, but she'd already read nearly half, so she couldn't abandon it either.

Radhika usually only locked the door at the bottom of the stairs when she went to bed. When she heard a light knock, she got up and noticed she'd been reading for over an hour. The door was slightly ajar. When she opened it, she found Akshay standing there.

'Come in,' she said, concealing her surprise.

Akshay entered and stood quietly for a moment. This was the first time he'd seen Radhika's room in a disordered state. The bedspread had been removed and thrown on the chair. Radhika's purse, handkerchief, and some newspapers had been placed on the other chair.

'Shall we sit outside?'

'No, I just came for a minute to say goodbye,' said Akshay, standing where he was.

When he'd entered the room, Radhika had the impression he had a great deal to say. Now, when he spoke, he sounded full of despair, but also annoyed. She could tell he'd changed his mind. She sat down on the takht and hugged the pillow.

'Akshay,' she said. 'Do sit a while. What's the hurry?'

Akshay sat down at the foot of the takht.

'Are you going away angry?'

'No, why would I be angry?' he asked with a slight grimace.

'That's how it seems.'

They both fell silent. There was a slight breeze and a piece of paper flapped on the roof.

'How did this sudden transfer come about?' asked Radhika, suppressing a sigh.

'It had been in the works for a while.'

'I'll think of you often.'

Radhika opened her book and shut it.

'Will you really?'

Radhika was irritated by the sarcasm Akshay's voice.

'You know I don't speak formally,' she said. 'Anyway, my circle of friends was already so small, and now...' she left the sentence unfinished. She saw that Akshay suddenly pressed his hand to his temple. 'You have a headache?' she asked softly.

'Yes, sometimes, when I get tired.'

Radhika got up and brought him water. She opened her purse, took out two Bufferin tablets, and placed them in Akshay's hand. Akshay swallowed the pills, then handed her back the glass. As Radhika turned to put the glass down, the buttery soft silk of her sari brushed against him. Akshay grabbed it without thinking. Radhika turned when she found herself unable to lean over to put away the glass. She was silent for a moment. Then she reached out and softly unclenched Akshay's fist to free her sari. She put down the glass and returned to sit on the takht near Akshay.

Akshay desired her. That was why he'd distanced himself. That was all it was. There was a long silence.

'How is the pain?' she asked softly.

'A lot less than before.' Akshay's throat felt tight.

A light breeze blew outside. Inside the room, it was growing dark, but because of the false roof of the room, a thin light filtered in, by which shapes could be discerned, but not facial expressions or emotions.

First, one of Akshay's shoes dropped to the floor with a thud. Then Radhika's book fell. Akshay took off his other shoe and placed it on the floor below.

Radhika turned over.

Some sounds rise to the surface in the darkness. Radhika felt sleepy, but many questions still spun about in Akshay's mind. He felt even sadder than before.

'You're feeling sleepy even today?'

Radhika laughed at his mournful tone.

'You should wake up; you have to leave early tomorrow morning, right?'

'Radhika truly, you are so...'

'Am I?' asked Radhika.

'I don't know how to talk sweetly.'

'You could try it without sweetness...' Radhika laughed.

'You'll just laugh.'

'Oh, now you're offended. Okay, I'm listening, tell me, what do you need to say?'

Akshay was trying to form his question properly.

'Do you still think about the past?' he asked.

Radhika covered her arms with the end of her sari. In the darkness, her voice sounded sad, but she replied steadily, 'What's the use of dwelling on the past? What I was then, I'm not now. I live life as it comes, and after that, I'm not the same as before. Tomorrow, too, after you leave, I'll...' she stopped.

'Radhika!' pleaded Akshay. 'Will you go with me? Will you live with me? I...you...' Radhika placed her hand on his lips.

'I don't want you to commit yourself in haste, Akshay,' she said.

A faint light shone in the east. When Radhika opened her eyes, she saw that Akshay had gone.

20

Radhika was put in the special guestroom this time, the one Papa always stayed in with Vidya when he came. When Vinay returned to Delhi this time, he insisted on bringing Radhika back with him. It was growing hotter by the day, and Radhika was wasting away in the upstairs room. Her skin was dry. Vinay never said much but he felt pleased when he saw Radhika. Radhika refused to come multiple times, but he would not listen. He wanted Radhika to pack up all her things and leave the house for good; she didn't even have much, not even enough to fill two large trunks. But Radhika refused. Though she agreed to come with him, it was on the condition that they wouldn't stop her from returning when she wanted.

'How have you been liking it here?' he asked, standing in the middle of the room. His servant, Bahadur, was packing up the luggage under Radhika's direction. She didn't reply. First the sunflower print came down and was packed up and put to one side. Then Radhika gathered up the smaller things, the hugachis, the engravings, the miniature bottle of Chianti. In just a short while the room was completely empty.

She rushed around busily, her palla stuffed in at the waist. She felt as though she'd only just now decorated the room with Sonam's help, and that Akshay would come directly from the office in the evening.

Akshay...Radhika's heart sank. Outside, the intense sunlight shimmered on the roof, the tree branches were still, and the clear sky outspread in a vast expanse. On these scorching days, her memories of that era of friendship rang false. It had been so long since Akshay's departure. In the beginning, Radhika had awaited his letters and phone calls with an eagerness that surprised her. After he'd left, she'd felt overwhelmed with sweetness for the first few weeks. Manish had also desired her, but Radhika had kept him at a distance. Despite feeling a strong physical attraction to him she'd remained in control, always reminding herself that Manish quickly tired of women. And after Dan, Radhika didn't wish to become another link in a chain for someone. She wanted to be the one and only empress, something which was only possible with Akshay. She felt respect for him, and with it a sort of pleasantness. She was impressed by his courteousness, and for this reason, discovering in him a moment of weakness—*no I'm not ashamed for him, but rather more desirous*, she thought—she kept probing her own feelings as she waited for him. She wasn't ashamed, not even for a moment, but as the gulf of silence between them grew, Radhika was vexed by the thought that she didn't really know how Akshay felt about her. And she was bewildered as well, at how little she knew him. She'd never tried to analyze him, even during the time they'd spent together. There was no need to know either; but why was she sinking into a gulf of darkness and despair?

Bhabhi was a bit surprised that Vinay had gone out of his way to look after Radhika, but she welcomed Radhika home nevertheless. Radhika was certainly surprised, but she knew how changeable Bhabhi was. When Bhabhi took her to the club a few times and introduced her America-returned sister-in-law with pride to her friends, Radhika understood she was merely a status symbol for her, just as the imported car in the portico was for Vinay.

Staying at Vinay's home was different for Radhika now. A large air conditioner ran in her room at all times of day. There was an attached study with empty bookcases, a reading desk and a swivel chair. A long lattice-covered veranda draped in budding yellow jasmine ran alongside the room. The gardener's wife would often plait the flowers into a garland for Radhika; Bahadur would arrange it on a silver tray and place it on Radhika's vanity table. There was a light breeze on the veranda in the evenings, and she'd bring out a chair and sit where she could see the trees laden with small mangoes and the carefully tended orchid stalks that grew in their shade. Vinay had always loved flowers, and even now, when an orchid bloomed, he would have it hung in Radhika's latticed veranda.

Vinay's business was booming. He had mills in Kanpur,

sugar factories in eastern UP, two cinema halls in town, and who knows what else? Eighteen karat diamonds sparkled in Bhabhi's ears. Yet, even amidst all this grandeur and wealth, Radhika was occasionally stung by unclear thoughts and felt overwhelmed by a strange agitation.

There was no one in the house to talk to, nor any companion for her; Bhabhi went early every morning to the beauty salon for an electric body massage, and Veena and Vivek went to school. The breakfast table was always piled high with food, and Vinay tried to get her to eat some of everything.

'You're getting thinner by the day,' he said one day. He folded up the newspaper, put it to one side, and stared at her.

'No, I'm not!'

'Do you eat ras bagaira?'

'Yes.' Radhika laughed softly.

It was Sunday, so the children were also at the table, and Bhabhi as well.

'Aunty lies in bed staring at the ceiling all day,' said Veena.

'And what else should I do all day?'

Radhika disliked being the focus of the conversation.

'Bhai, our home does not suit her. When she came back from spending two days at Rajju's home, her face sparkled,' said Bhabhi.

Vinay and Bhabhi both looked at Radhika. She felt a sudden rush of anger, but held it in.

'You are right, Bhabhi, today I'm going back to Rajju

Mama's house. And I'm only returning when my face begins to sparkle.'

Vinay placed some apple slices on her plate. 'Eat properly,' he said.

Radhika got up from the breakfast table and went to her room. So Bhabhi had finally reverted to form, or, as the English say, 'Can the leopard change its spots?' And then she cried angry tears, wondering why she had come here. Vinay thought all she needed to achieve in life was to eat fruit, drink juice, and sometimes go out for a drive.

Nowadays, Radhika often turned her life over and over to examine it, coldly critiquing her own emotions. On this soft bed and in this house stuffed with creature comforts, she contemplated how long-lasting human bonds are, and how quickly people forget them. She thought about Bhabhi, who in her obsession with becoming the mistress of several mills had forgotten all else. Did she not feel lonely inside? And did she really believe all the flattery of the sycophants that milled about her? And Veena, who from the time of her birth to the present moment had never seen hunger, poverty, lack of medicines, or crowded hospitals; could she ever truly understand the emotions of others less fortunate than herself? And she wondered the same thing about herself, for if she had, she wouldn't have had such an immature reaction to Papa's wedding.

Yes, in those days, Radhika had been over-emotional and impetuous. She'd never given a moment's thought to the loneliness in Papa's life. By leaving Papa and going to live with Dan, Radhika had acquired several years of experience and matured quickly. Only then had she had the courage to part from Dan. *Now I'm free*, she thought. *Mature too. I can forge my own life, my own future.*

She thought of Akshay again for a moment. Suddenly, a vision of the future came to her, and she realized that now Akshay was gone from her life for good. Time had come in waves and washed away his name, and one day it would wash away altogether the memory of his heated breaths and tight embrace. Until that happened, Radhika would do anything. She would go to one of those schools that had opened for Tibetan refugees, where people came from far away to teach, simply out of the spirit of service and to live an exceptionally simple life. Was this an escape, she wondered. No, this was not escape, it was a struggle. She would finally be free of this suffocation and this boring prison.

21

She took a rickshaw and went to Rajju Mama's house that very day. When she arrived, she found that Rajju Mama had gone to take part in a family wedding; only Nani was at home. The last time she'd come, Nani had been staying with Radhika's other uncle, but now Mausi was at that house and Nani was here.

Radhika noticed that Nani had lost all her teeth and come to look quite elderly and tired in just the past three or four years. She sat by the brazier, stirring some halwa with a ladle, sometimes stopping to glance at Radhika.

Radhika sat silently nearby, lost in thought, though she was not unaware of the atmosphere around her. Nani had pulled the end of her sari over her head, and Radhika could see it had been patched in several spots. The kitchen hadn't been painted for quite some time either. There was a small grinding stone, a few pots, and some mismatched plates and katoris in one corner. Nani was alone in the house at that moment; Rajju Mama would return the next day. She was making halwa for Radhika's breakfast. The whole kitchen was fragrant with the aroma of semolina roasting in ghee. Radhika sat on a low stool with her back to the wall. She had told Nani not to go to the trouble several times, but Nani wouldn't listen. Outside in the courtyard stood Nani's bamboo charpoy, loaded up with fruit, two boxes of sweets and two dozen bottles of Coca Cola, all brought by Radhika.

'You must have brought all this from Vinay's home?' Nani asked softly.

'No, Nani, I bought it in the bazaar.'

'So then...' Nani said, 'if you're spending so much money, who's giving it to you? Your Papa?'

'No one is. I bought it all myself.'

'You saved all this money and brought it back with you?' asked Nani with surprise.

Radhika smiled slightly. 'I saved enough for a year's expenses.'

'And now you've spent it all.' Nani threw a bit of burnt semolina to one side. 'Vinay can't even make enough to take care of his sister's expenses—even when he's hoarding black market rupees.'

'What are you talking about Nani?' asked Radhika. 'Vinay...'

'I know everything. The whole city knows. The black market is everywhere nowadays.'

Nani braced her back with her hand and stood up with a small moan.

'My back is all bent over, did you see? After all I'm sixty-eight.' Nani tottered over to the cabinet and began taking out the cups.

'I won't drink tea, it's too hot today,' said Radhika 'You sit down, I'll do everything.' She insisted on seating Nani on the charpoy and brought a teapoy out into the courtyard. Nani had made the halwa very sweet. After eating a couple of spoonfuls, Radhika slipped her dish under the teapoy and began cutting up fruit. Nani tasted a few slices of mango.

'The taste hasn't come yet.'

'The melon is sweet, try that,' said Radhika.

'Shall I eat fruit, or barfi?' asked Nani.

'No, try this, Nani, it's milk pudding.'

'This is the first time I'm eating this,' said Nani as she savoured it. 'It tastes a bit like barfi made from moong dal.'

~

The evening sun slanted into the courtyard, a breeze whispered through the dried jujube bush, and a radio played next door. A lock of white hair fell across Nani's forehead. Radhika and Nani were both drinking Coca Cola. Radhika from the bottle and Nani from a tin cup.

'Tell me, dear, there must be lots of Coca Cola there?'

'Yes!'

'Sometimes, the children bring it home. Last year the little one insisted I drink it.'

'Well, then, you must drink all these bottles.'

'Arre, all this hardly interests me in old age. It's just that if you only eat plain food, sometimes you want a little something different,' Nani said simply. She fell silent.

There was a knock on the outside door. A car had come to fetch Radhika.

'I wanted to stay the night,' said Radhika, when she returned.

'But where would you sleep? Bahu has locked up her room. You'd be uncomfortable in my little room. It's hot and there are mosquitoes.'

Radhika sat back down. She didn't wish to return, but she knew that if she insisted on staying, Nani would fret about her.

'All right, I'll leave,' said Radhika.

The two of them sat silently.

'Is Vinay looking for a boy for you?'

Radhika was startled to hear this question in the darkness. She laughed, 'I don't know.'

'Or you yourself will look?'

'Who would marry me?' asked Radhika, but not out of seriousness, only for Nani's sympathy. Nani sighed deeply and put down her glass.

'Look, your fate will dictate what happens. I keep worrying. I want it to happen when I'm still here; then I'll be at peace. Your mother died young, and no one even arranged Vinay's wedding. So there's just you. I've kept a couple of things set aside for you,' said Nani tearfully.

'Really? What are they?'

'Arre, nothing special, really. But the bahus don't know. I have your Nana's kurta buttons and an armlet for you.'

Nani let out a sob.

'Have another Coca Cola,' said Radhika, 'before they get warm.'

'All right, bring me one,' said Nani.

'You must remember our haveli in the village, Radhika,' said Nani. 'Now there's nothing left. I've heard they've opened a government school there. Your Papa's baraat arrived there with such fanfare. There were three dancing girls from Kanpur and people were packed in from all the surrounding villages. Your Baba was also a generous man, very generous! It was as though silver showered down on your mother that day. But fate had other plans. She only managed to live four or five years after that. And now, of course, the world has changed. The land is gone, the property is gone, we even had to sell our ancestral haveli. In the rebellion of '57, a battalion gathered outside that haveli. There must still be a few of the guns left.'

The radio had grown softer, only a few scattered stars shone in the sky, the jujube bush was now peaceful and still, and the fragrance of the nearby flowering vines filled the courtyard. Somewhere a bell chimed nine o'clock.

'Arre, it's got so late. Now you should go. They must be waiting for you at Vinay's.' Nani stumbled and stood up. She motioned to Radhika to come with her into her room, where she unlocked the almirah and took out an old handkerchief. There were two eight-anna pieces in it. She gave them to Radhika and said, 'Take these. After all, you brought things with you.'

'Nani, why would I take money for any of that?' asked Radhika angrily. Such stillness there was all around.

'Arre, what does it matter? I don't like taking money from a daughter. This is all I have saved in my old age.'

Radhika picked up one eight-anna piece and clenched it in her fist, 'All right, then this is enough,' she said.

Nani didn't insist too much. She tied the handkerchief back up and stuffed it into a corner, relocked the almirah, and accompanied Radhika back outside.

'Kahari will come to sleep here at night. Don't worry,' said Nani.

Radhika sat down in the car clutching the eight-anna piece tightly in her fist like an amulet.

'Come and visit over there sometimes, won't you?'

'If they send a car, I'll come,' Nani replied with a toothless laugh.

The car set off.

22

Radhika spent countless days in that dark room nestled in the soft mattress. Slowly she grew accustomed to the uneventful daily routine, just as she had to lying alone on the takht in her flat. The air conditioner ran at all times. Vinay came in periodically to ask how she was doing. Veena was busy getting ready to go to the hills with Bhabhi and soon there would be a film premier at the Veena featuring some famous stars. For a week, Veena had been busy coming up with the perfect outfit for the occasion. Vinay wanted Radhika to come as well.

The morning of the premier, Radhika received a call from Manish. He wanted to see her.

'Okay, come over,' said Radhika.

After hanging up, she stood for quite a while on the veranda. Life without men was certainly dull, but it was also free of worry, and Radhika had started to find that rather enjoyable. Now Manish would come and upset the balance again. What did he want? He had no shortage of friends or girlfriends. So why did he keep bothering Radhika? Was it because she'd said there was no room in her life for a person like him?

By evening, Radhika had started to feel excited, perhaps because she was getting bored of her uneventful life. And she might actually enjoy spending an evening with Manish.

When she came out of her room, Manish had already arrived. Vinay's son had seated him in the formal drawing room. Radhika came in smiling and Manish stood up when he saw her.

'What brings you here?' she asked.

'I had some work here,' he replied briefly, gazing at Radhika. She wore a pale organdy sari and had decorated her hair with yellow flowers. She shrank back in Manish's gaze. 'Come, let's sit outside,' she said, and they went out to sit on the lawn.

The lawn smelled of fragrant earth and freshly cut grass. Manish's complexion had tanned; perhaps he'd been working in the sun for several weeks. This time, he'd come stylishly dressed in a suit and tie.

'How did you find my address?' asked Radhika, lightly tapping the arm of the chair with her fingernails.

'I went by your flat and learned you weren't there. The people downstairs had also gone to Calcutta.'

'To Calcutta?' Radhika blurted out.

'Yes, to Akshay's. Deki went too. The Pahari was there. It was from him that I heard you'd silently slipped away without telling me.'

'Vinay wouldn't listen,' Radhika said quietly. 'And what are you up to?'

'Some of our researchers are on a dig in Rajasthan and Gujarat along an old trade route—I was over there.'

Vinay came outside as well, and Radhika introduced him. He looked Manish over carefully, then sat next to him. After that, Bhabhi came out, and then Veena.

'You two must come tonight too,' insisted Veena. 'You will come, yes?'

Radhika looked at Manish. He laughed slightly, and said, 'If your aunty is going then I'll go too. I haven't seen a film in ages.'

Radhika agreed to go, concealing a sense of hopelessness. Vinay now felt at ease and leaned back in his chair. He called to the servant to bring drinks; beer for him and Manish, pineapple juice for Radhika and Coca Cola for Bhabhi and Veena.

'Where is Karen?' she asked, so there would be no false notions about their relationship.

'She's in Pakistan these days; she's probably on her way back now,' said Manish.

They sat out on the lawn until it was time to go to the show. Bhabhi seemed impressed with Manish. Radhika and Manish brought Veena with them. Veena sat between them and Radhika felt irritable at the sight of her radiant face. She felt rather fatigued herself.

Manish returned the next evening as well and stayed for dinner on Bhabhi's insistence.

On the third day, they were allowed to go out alone. Veena was dying to go with them, but Vinay stopped her. Nonetheless, it was decided that Manish would have dinner at their house afterwards. They went out for coffee in Hazratganj first, then strolled about for a while.

'This is the first time I've been in Lucknow in ages,' said Manish.

'So how does it look?'

'The way Delhi did to you.'

'Dull and dark,' said Radhika.

'As a child, the Imambara and the other old buildings seemed huge to me. But now, even the pyramid looks depressing,' remarked Radhika after a little while.

They walked all the way down the street and reached Manish's car.

Manish drove around aimlessly for a while, then stopped in a deserted area. A breeze blew in through the windows bearing the fragrance of some unknown flower. The light of the Shaheed Smarak glimmered far off.

Radhika sat silently in her seat.

'For three days I've been looking for some peace and quiet to talk with you.'

'Talk! About what?' asked Radhika.

Two cyclists rode by staring at the parked car.

'Why are you sitting so far away?'

She slid across the seat to be closer to Manish. She knew she wanted him to take her in his arms, but she also knew that if he did, she would protest, open the door, and get out if he didn't listen to her. And it occurred to her that it would be hard to find a rickshaw around here.

'Radhika, I've decided I won't go back.'

Radhika was startled in the darkness by Manish's serious tone, but she didn't let it show.

'How did you decide that so suddenly?' she asked, laughing slightly to lighten the mood.

'It's not at all sudden; I've thought about this quite a bit. If I'd stayed abroad a few more years, it would have become impossible for me to return to India, and I don't want to live permanently abroad.'

'But can you be happy living in India?' she asked lightly.

'Maybe not at first, but I'll try.'

'What about Karen?' she asked, adjusting her sari border.

'Karen doesn't want to settle in India...I won't mourn her for long,' Manish replied easily.

Radhika bit her tongue to stop herself from responding bitterly. She turned her head away and gazed outside into the darkness.

Manish was silent a while as he awaited her reaction. 'What are you thinking?' he asked.

'What should I say? Whatever you think best,' she said. 'What will you do if you stay?'

'It'll take several years to get this institute up and running, so I can stay on for some time, not as the director but as an advisor.'

Radhika felt Manish was making a mistake. In a short while, once his enthusiasm for the project had waned, he would probably grow bored. It wasn't in his nature to stay tied down; he had a self-willed, nomadic nature.

'It seems as though you're not especially happy about it,' said Manish.

'What does my happiness have to do with it? Manish, where do I even enter your life?' asked Radhika coolly.

Manish turned to look at her.

'How long will you think that way, Radhika?' he asked. 'How long will you keep rejecting me?'

She was about to speak, but he stopped her.

'No, don't say anything. I want you to take some time to think about it! There's a camaraderie between the two of us, an easiness in our relations. I will accept you totally: your moods, your problems, your past.' He hesitated, 'But have you already accepted Akshay?'

'No. Don't drag Akshay into this,' Radhika blurted out in an injured tone.

'But you and Akshay...' Manish spoke so softly, then fell silent. His words would have been inaudible but for the stillness. He held her fists in his hands. He couldn't see her eyes welling with tears.

Radhika wanted to say, *I would have given Akshay everything if he'd accepted me,* but she knew she could say this to no one.

Manish must have suspected what she was feeling. He passed his hand over her eyelids. They were wet.

'You couldn't stay over there, nor are you accepted here. I too find myself apart. I thought the two of us could stay together because we've known each other a long time, in many different contexts...but if you...' Manish sounded sad.

Radhika lifted her head. Manish's face wasn't visible in the twilight. She'd never seen him sad. Always in a cheerful mask. A popular, sociable, successful man. Now he let go of Radhika's hand. He rested his arm on the steering wheel and searched for a cigarette in his pocket.

Manish lit a cigarette and took a few puffs. 'If I say something, will you listen?' he asked. 'I'm taking a few people to Khajuraho. Will you join us? All the arrangements have already been made; you'll be quite comfortable. I'd like it if you came. We'd sit together in the evenings and chat.'

Many thoughts rose in Radhika's mind—beautiful Khajuraho evenings, a quiet dak bungalow, Manish. She shook her head, and said, 'That might not be possible.'

'I was expecting you to say that,' he said. 'But think about it, I'll save a space for you...'

A silence overshadowed them again. Radhika patted her hair flat. 'Come, they must be waiting for us at dinner,' she said.

On their way back, she stared out into the darkness, at the closed stores, the darkened signboards, a few paan sellers here and there.

Manish said nothing more either. When they returned, surrounded by Vinay, Bhabhi, and the rest of the family, he again became the perfect guest, full of charm. He accepted a drink from Vinay and turned towards Bhabhi to listen to her conversation.

Radhika was exhausted. She was silent during dinner. Only Vinay and Manish conversed during dinner, and after it was over, Manish expressed his gratitude and took his leave. When he was about to go, Bhabhi said to Radhika, 'Do accompany him outside.'

Radhika stood up and walked with him to the gate.

'I've exhausted you,' said Manish sadly. 'Were you bored as well?'

'Of course not.' Radhika felt embarrassed by her rudeness. 'When will you come again?' she asked.

'Now it's up to you to come to me,' replied Manish. He tried to reach out and touch her shoulders, but she moved away, murmuring, 'Darbaan is standing right over there.'

Manish left.

23

So this idol too had been smashed.

Radhika stood in the doorway staring at Papa. Dusk had fallen in the room, but the dim light of evening shone through the window where Papa sat. The study had been locked up for quite some time, and now it smelled close and musty. Papa had been sitting there for the past week, staring steadily outside. It rained frequently. The coral vine that hung from the wires drooped in the rain, along with the crepe myrtle outside Vidya's bedroom.

How jarring the colours looked now; usually these flowers had looked lovely in the rain. Only the context had changed.

Papa glanced up at Radhika.

'Papa—soup!'

'Come, sit.' He sat with his feet stretched out on the couch. Papa pulled up his feet and Radhika sat down.

He stared at Radhika for a while. She wore a white sari with a thin border and had pulled her hair back in a bun. She felt weary.

'The soup is ready...' Radhika said softly.

'I'll have it in a bit.'

Radhika could not look at Papa. Now when she sat by him, she felt as though her breath had stopped and she was suffocating. She wanted to get up and run but she sat immobile, doing nothing.

How empty this house was now, and how sad it felt. First Radhika had left for abroad, then Papa had departed for the house across the Ganga, and now, Vidya!

No one had openly wept for Vidya. Even Papa's eyes remained dry. Somehow it didn't feel as though Vidya was no more. All around were marks of her presence: the colours on the walls, the curtains, the false ceiling; only Vidya's bedroom lay empty. Papa always sat on the couch in his attached study. He must also be sleeping there at night. Radhika stared at her feet. Rama had been unable to come, due to impending childbirth. Vidya had no other close relations. The suddenness of the news had laid Bhabhi up in bed, and Papa was completely silent. Vinay was looking after the outside tasks and Radhika had immediately thrown herself into the inside tasks. Things had reverted somewhat to the pre-Vidya days. But several bitter years had passed in the interim, and Vidya too. Now there was no Vidya, but the memory of those years which had been endured remained, even if they'd left no traces on Radhika.

Radhika didn't want to look at Papa. In the midst of all this, she was surprised at how her emotions had become so dulled that she felt very little at all.

She could not put on a show like Bhabhi had: weeping,

singing, sighing deeply, and lying in bed as though she'd been deeply attached to Vidya. Perhaps Papa had also come to feel disgusted by this, because he hadn't once asked after Bhabhi's health.

By now the room had completely filled with darkness. A few mosquitoes had started to buzz about. Water poured down in an uneven stream from the drain on the roof into a small tank.

Ideas return in silence. It felt as though that night had occurred at some time in the distant past. She hadn't been able to sleep for a long time after bidding farewell to Manish. She'd known him in many contexts, but after coming to India, she'd seen something new in him. Who knew if he would be happy staying here permanently.

Radhika felt dejected. Her thoughts buzzed with Manish, and now she had the sensation of a thousand ants crawling over her unsatiated body. She kept finding herself whisking them away with her hand. Lying awake for so long was agitating her. She washed her face with cold water, then took a red sleeping pill and lay down. She slept until late the next morning.

When she awoke, the tea placed on the teapoy by her bed had gone cold. A thin, repulsive skin had formed over it. She'd asked several times that tea not be brought to her already prepared. She dragged herself out of bed; she would take a sleeping pill to make herself cheerful. She still clung to these tiny conveniences from that foreign civilization.

She had stood for a long time under a cold stream of water. Then a tapping started on the bathroom door. It must be a phone call from Manish.

'What is it?' she called.

'Just come outside.' It was Vinay.

Radhika wiped off her body, put on her clothes, wrapped her wet hair in a towel, and came out.

Vinay was pacing about. She stopped when she saw him. Without any preamble, he blurted out, 'Papa called. Vidya's overdosed on sleeping pills...'

Radhika stared at him, stunned.

'He's taken her to the hospital.'

Radhika suddenly found words to speak. 'Vidya did? Why? Was she troubled?'

Vinay gave her a meaningful glance but quickly controlled himself.

Radhika sat down on the foot of the bed. Her legs were shaking.

'Papa called? He was across the Ganga, wasn't he?'

'I didn't have time to ask all that. He spoke haltingly and softly.'

'We should go, Vinay. Papa's alone.' Radhika stood up.

'I've told the driver to get the car ready,' said Vinay.

Radhika began drying her hair. She too had taken a sleeping pill the night before. Perhaps Vidya had taken them one at a time, knowing that she didn't want to see morning again. Why had she felt that way? She recalled Vidya's chilly, controlled face. Would she survive? And what about Papa...!

The journey had taken several hours. The old driver drove with steady hands. Vinay dozed between the jolts of the road. Radhika stared unblinking out the window, terrified. Bhabhi had not come along; she would come later. So there was no one there to interrupt Radhika's thoughts.

By the time they'd arrived, it had been early evening. The wind sighed and there was a dim light on in the portico. Radhika went and stood in the sitting room. Papa started and looked up; he saw Vinay standing behind Radhika.

'You both came!' he said.

No one liked to ask what had happened. Their aunt was there, with her family and some other distant relations.

'She was so intelligent, who knows how she accidentally took so many sleeping pills,' lamented their aunt.

Radhika didn't reply.

The darkness in every corner gaped as though ready to swallow the pomegranate trees shading the courtyard. Vidya had lived alone in this place for so long. Radhika had never made a proper attempt to get to know her. She'd always remained in the grip of prejudice, and now Papa seemed so helpless: timid and broken. Radhika could not sit in that room. She felt like a house shaken to its foundations after an earthquake. As though the walls had cracked...

One week had passed in this manner. An Assamese bedspread covered Vidya's bed. No one knew what Papa was feeling.

'Papa, shall I turn on the lights?' she asked.

Papa seemed startled by her voice. 'If you want to, otherwise, no...'

A firefly had slipped into the room. It flew about in circles, flickering.

'Vinay and everyone, are they leaving tomorrow?' asked Papa in a formal tone.

'They were saying that.'

'And you, dear?'

Radhika took a deep breath. Papa leaned over and placed a hand on her shoulder. Radhika suddenly melted from that touch. Her nostrils flared slightly. She bit her lips. She tried to control her emotions.

'And you, Papa?'

'I haven't thought about myself at all. I want you to stay here, Radhika, like before.'

Radhika was relieved that Papa's face was not visible in the darkness.

'No, Papa I want to leave. Manish...a friend of mine...' she stopped mid-sentence.

Papa withdrew his hand. He leaned back against his cushion.

Perhaps he too had begun to watch the firefly careening about the room.

ALSO IN SPEAKING TIGER

FIFTY-FIVE PILLARS, RED WALLS

Usha Priyamvada

Translated from the Hindi by Daisy Rockwell

'[A] wonderful writer...one of the few Hindi writers to have consistently and sensitively chronicled women's lives... Priyamvada expertly examines the loneliness of lives outside the socially comfortable zones of marriage and motherhood.' —Poonam Saxena, *The Hindustan Times*

First published in 1961, Usha Priyamvada's debut novel *Pachpan Khambe, Laal Deewaarein* is located within the boundaries of an all-women's college in Delhi. Behind its walls is Sushma Sharma—lecturer, warden, single, and sole provider for her large family. Despite her relative youth and elegance, she is resigned to the regimented loneliness of her life, until a chance meeting with the charismatic Neel. Then, long-thwarted desires uncurl and the shackles she has accepted suddenly begin to seem unbearable. But the world around her is still unchanged, and independence still causes scandal...

In spare, evocative prose, *Fifty-five Pillars, Red Walls* skilfully explores the physical, mental and social paradigms which locked so many women into narrow ideals, as they still do. Daisy Rockwell's pitch-perfect translation brings this quietly intense, poignant and pathbreaking Hindi novel into the blazing spotlight of classic Indian literature for the first time.